"Mercy, look at me," Tony insisted.

"I am," she said, unable to stop thinking about his muscular chest, his strong arms. . . .

"No, you're not. You're talking to my shirt."

She knew his chest would be gorgeous, covered with dark, curly hair, and his arms would reach for her, gather her close—

"Look at me, Mercy. Keep your eyes looking at my eyes—you can do that, can't you?"

"I don't think that's such a terrific idea," she said softly.

He moved closer to her, and her gaze rose to his face. "Why isn't it a good idea? Because you felt what I did when I opened the door? You did feel it, didn't you? That same desire we felt when we first met, growing stronger and stronger? How long did we stand there, Mercy? Do you know?"

"Tony," she whispered. "Don't."

"Something strange happens every time we look at each other. I want to know what's going on."

"Well, how am I supposed to know?" she exclaimed. "I'm not in the habit of being unable to move because some big lummox is hypnotizing me, or whatever, with the darkest, most mesmerizing eyes I've ever seen. And I usually don't fantasize about what it would be like to . . . to . . ."

Her voice trailed off, and a warm flush of embarrassment stained her cheeks. "Erase all that. Those words were never spoken. I didn't say them, so you didn't hear them."

Suddenly she was in his arms, and she knew every word was true. . . .

WHAT ARE *LOVESWEPT* ROMANCES?

They are stories of true romance and touching emotion. We believe those two very important ingredients are constants in our highly sensual and very believable stories in the *LOVESWEPT* line. Our goal is to give you, the reader, stories of consistently high quality that may sometimes make you laugh, sometimes make you cry, but are always fresh and creative and contain many delightful surprises within their pages.

Most romance fans read an enormous number of books. Those they truly love, they keep. Others may be traded with friends and soon forgotten. We hope that each *LOVESWEPT* romance will be a treasure—a "keeper." We will always try to publish

*LOVE STORIES YOU'LL NEVER FORGET
BY AUTHORS YOU'LL ALWAYS REMEMBER*

The Editors

Loveswept 534

Joan Elliott Pickart
Night Magic

BANTAM BOOKS
NEW YORK · TORONTO · LONDON · SYDNEY · AUCKLAND

NIGHT MAGIC
A Bantam Book / April 1992

If you would be interested in receiving protective vinyl
covers for your Loveswept books, please write to this address
for information:

Loveswept
Bantam Books
P.O. Box 985
Hicksville, NY 11802

ISBN 0-553-44236-8

Published simultaneously in the United States and Canada

Bantam Books are published by Bantam Books, a division of
Bantam Doubleday Dell Publishing Group, Inc. Its trademark,
consisting of the words "Bantam Books" and the portrayal of
a rooster, is Registered in U.S. Patent and Trademark Office
and in other countries. Marca Registrada. Bantam Books, 666
Fifth Avenue, New York, New York 10103.

PRINTED IN THE UNITED STATES OF AMERICA

OPM   0 9 8 7 6 5 4 3 2 1

FOR G.M.

One

Her life, Mercy Sloan often mused, revolved rather strangely around the number four.

She was the fourth child to be born to Fred and Bertie Sloan.

She had arrived on the fourth day, of the fourth month, at 4:04 A.M.

For as long as she could remember, things happened to her in clusters of fours. Sometimes they were good, sometimes they were bad, but there were definitely four, not the superstitious three that everyone spoke of.

Often weeks would pass without a total of four of anything happening. But just when Mercy began to think that maybe the jinx, or whatever it was, was at long last over, four something-or-others would occur, and she could only sigh as her hopes died.

So, it came as no surprise to her when she awakened that morning to hear the sound of rain beating against the windows.

That it was pouring, she reasoned, as she yawned away the fogginess of sleep, was a given. It had rained steadily for the past three days, this was day four, therefore . . .

She showered, dressed in khaki slacks with a matching belted camp jacket, ate a bowl of cereal and a slice of toast while consuming two cups of coffee, and prepared to leave the apartment.

As soon as she stepped outside, her umbrella fell apart. It didn't stick for a moment when she pressed the button, then pop open as it should. It didn't refuse to budge. It simply fell apart, as neat as you please, two pieces landing on the sidewalk, the plastic handle still clutched in her fingers.

"That," she said, frowning as she dropped the three sections of the umbrella in a dumpster, "is one."

She ran to the parking area next to her apartment building, splashing through puddles and feeling her clothes become waterlogged. Being a pro at counting to four disasters, she knew she could not chalk up getting drenched as number two. No, being soaked was part of the umbrella bit. There was no fooling the goblins who kept the tally. Not a chance.

Inside her blue compact car she shivered, then turned the key in the ignition. The motor purred instantly, and she flicked on the windshield wipers. They sprang to life and then . . .

"Oh, my Lord," she exclaimed.

One windshield wiper flew off in one direction, the other was airborne the opposite way. In seconds they were gone, disappearing into a swirling haze of windblown rain.

"Aaak!" Mercy yelled in frustration, then drew a steadying breath. Calm down, she told herself. A tantrum was not going to solve the dilemma of rocket-propelled windshield wipers. But one thing was for certain. "That's two," she said decisively, as she got out of the car. "That is most definitely two."

She trudged back through the puddles to her apartment, and packed clothes from undies on out in a canvas tote bag. Then, as though it were a perfectly reasonable thing to do, she strolled to the bus stop at the corner, smiling at the people she passed, who eyed her warily.

When she entered the one-story building that housed Sloan Nursery and Landscaping, she glared murderously at the three occupants of the office in the back, daring them to speak. Her soaked shoes squished a merry tune as she crossed the room. No one spoke.

A few minutes later she emerged from the

bathroom in gray slacks and a green cotton sweater.

"Good morning," she sang out. "How's everyone this lovely morning in Santa Barbara, California? Clark? Drew? Phil? Are we all happy campers today?"

"As the eldest of the Sloan offspring," her brother Phil said, "I'll put my life on the line for my siblings. Why, little sister, did you choose to swim to work?"

"I don't wish to discuss it, thank you," Mercy said, lifting her chin.

"What's the count?" Drew asked.

She sat down at her desk. "Two."

"Damn." Clark tossed his pencil onto the blotter on top of his own desk. "Could you run through three and four before our lunch meeting today? This will be a plum job if we get it. We're talking megabucks here. No offense, Mercy, but . . ."

"Don't worry about a thing," she said, waving one hand breezily in the air. "My preliminary presentation is prepared, Clark, and we'll impress the socks off . . . whatever his name is."

"Murretti," Clark said. "Anthony Murretti."

"A tad Italian," Drew said.

Clark nodded. "No doubt about it. Which reminds me. When I met Tony at his office two weeks ago, I noticed some sharp oil paintings of Italy on his walls. I have a feeling they didn't come from K mart. He's a good-looking guy, too, a little over six feet tall and in good shape. He moves like an athlete. You know, smooth, controlled."

"What are you?" Drew asked. "President of the Tony Murretti fan club?"

"No, idiot," Clark said. "I'm just saying that I like the guy. He's not arrogant rich; he's sure-of-who-he-is-and-what-he-wants rich. I wouldn't cross him, though. I got the very distinct impression that Tony Murretti doesn't allow anyone to push him against the wall."

"So don't push him," Phil said. "Just get his name on the dotted line on one of our contracts."

"It's a little early for that," Clark said. "With any luck, though, Mercy and I will make progress at lunch today. I'd still feel better if you had disasters three and four before we go, Mercy."

"Hush," she said. "One and two were so grim, I should get double credit for each. Maybe I did, and all four are taken care of."

"Somehow I don't think so," Phil said. "It's never worked that way in the past."

Mercy sighed. "True."

"Murretti isn't married," Clark said. "He'd be a real catch, but he's too old for you, Mercy. He's at least thirty-five."

Mercy straightened in her chair. "He's not too old for me. I'm twenty-five, if you'll recall."

"No, he's not the one for you," Clark said,

shaking his head. "I figure Tony has been around the block a few times. He's got class, but . . . It's hard to explain. He's got this way of looking at you that's unnerving. His eyes are so dark, you can't see the pupils, and he never flinches, just stares directly at you. Forget it, Mercy, he's not for you."

"Clark, you're doing it again," Mercy said. "I've told all three of you a hundred times that I'll tend to my own love life. Phil, as the only married member of this menagerie, would you inform your brothers to worry about getting wives for themselves and leave the finding of my future husband to me?"

"Mercy said to—" Phil began.

"Oh, be quiet," she said, laughing. "Get to work."

As the three grinning men turned back to their tasks, Mercy looked at each one, smiling with love.

She adored her brothers, Phil, Drew, and Clark, ages thirty-four, thirty-two, and thirty. They were all big, strong, handsome men, and they would wrap her in cotton and protect her from the world if she'd allow it.

She and her brothers all had dark brown eyes, and Phil and Drew also had brown hair, like their father. Clark and Mercy had inherited the dark auburn shade of their mother's hair, except from out of nowhere Mercy had been dished up a gene that made her hair naturally curly.

Mercy gazed at her brothers a moment longer, then pulled a folder toward her and flipped it open.

"Mercy?" Clark said.

"Yes?" she said, not looking at him.

"Your hair is going boing."

She blinked, then slowly turned her head to look at Clark. "Pardon me?"

"Good-bye, Clark," Phil muttered. "We'll attend your funeral, unless we've got something else scheduled."

"What I mean is," Clark said, ignoring Phil, "it was dripping wet when you came in, now it's dry, and your curls sort of look like bedsprings sticking up and going boing. I just thought I'd mention it because we're having lunch with Tony Mur—Oh, boy, I know that expression. You're mad as hell."

Mercy got to her feet, pursed her lips, grabbed her purse, then spun around and marched across the room to the bathroom. The slamming of the door reverberated through the office.

"What did I do?" Clark asked, turning to his brothers. "What in the hell did I do? All I said was—"

"Clark, Clark," Phil said, shaking his head. "My son, you're hopeless. Don't get married . . .

ever. I'd go broke buying sympathy cards for your poor wife."

Drew dissolved in a fit of laughter. Clark glared at Phil. Phil sighed with great melodrama.

In the bathroom Mercy brushed, combed, tugged, and pushed at her hair.

Clark was right, she realized. Her hair was going boing. She was a week overdue for a trim, and this was the price she was going to pay for procrastination. Boinging hair, for Pete's sake. She was a combination of Shirley Temple, Raggedy Ann, and Orphan Annie.

"Drat," she said, and gave her wayward curls one final flick with the brush. "Oh! Oh! Ow!" she yelped, in the next instant. She dropped the brush and covered her right eye with one hand. Bending over, she popped out a contact lens and blinked her watering eye.

By closing her right eye and peering at the lens in her palm, she could barely see the jagged scratch on the contact. A bristle of the hairbrush, she guessed, must have snapped off and whipped across the lens. She'd have to make an appointment with her optometrist to determine if the lens could be buffed, or if a new one would have to be ordered.

"Hello to thee," she said dryly, "number three."

She popped out the other lens, then, holding

her contact case nearly to her nose, put the pair in the case.

Her tortoiseshell glasses were buried at the bottom of her purse. She dug them out and shoved them into place, dreading the moment when she'd view her reflection in the mirror. She knew what was waiting for her, and as she slowly lifted her gaze, she allowed a groan of disgust to erupt and echo in the small bathroom.

"Oh, yuck," she said aloud.

Around the nosepiece of the glasses was a lump of adhesive tape holding the frame together, where it had been split neatly in half when she had sat on the glasses.

That had been several weeks before, she recalled, the number two of a bad series of four that had ended with a root canal.

She was now, she realized dismally, going to have to impress the ever-so-important Tony Murretti while looking like a kid who'd been in a brawl on the playground.

"Wonderful," she said under her breath as she left the bathroom. "Just wonderful."

She sat back down at her desk, adopted what she hoped was a nonchalant expression, and waited, teeth clenched, for Clark to look at her.

"Mercy, where is—Holy Hannah, what's that glop on your nose?"

Mercy sighed. Clark had looked at her.

Phil glanced over at his sister. "I'd say it's adhesive tape."

"Yep," Drew said. "That's what it is, all right. Mercy's glasses have a boo-boo."

"Cute," Clark said, getting to his feet. "Mercy, tell me you plan to put your contacts back in before we go to lunch."

"Oh, well, I . . ." Mercy started, carefully examining the fingernails of one hand. "Do you like this shade of polish? It's called 'Chilled Watermelon.' Delicious, huh? I think it's very—"

"Mercy!"

She jumped to her feet, whirling to face Clark. At five feet five inches and wearing low-heeled shoes, she had to tilt her head back to meet and match his stormy expression.

"No, Mr. Sloan," she said, her fists planted on her hips, "I am not putting my contacts back in because one is scratched. That's disaster three of the four. If you don't stop hollering at me, number four will probably be my breaking my hand when I punch your nose. Got that?"

"What I've got," Clark said, "is a headache." He peered at her. "You remind me of someone wearing glasses and a phony rubber nose, only you lost the nose somewhere. There is no way, Mercy Sloan, that you're sitting across the table from Tony Murretti with that wad of tape on your face."

"Your ball, Mercy," Phil said.

"Clark," Mercy said, ignoring Phil. "I can't see

anything up close without my glasses or contacts. It's all a blur. You know that."

"We'll wing it," Clark said. "You can't wear those glasses. We're trying to impress Murretti. What will he think when he sees one of the Sloans is obviously too broke to have her glasses repaired? You'll blow our image of an up-and-coming landscaping outfit straight to hell." He shook his head. "No, you're not wearing those things."

"Fine, Clark," Mercy said, fluttering her eyelashes at him. "Whatever you say, Clark. I'll take off my glasses the moment we step inside the restaurant. Phil? Drew? You are witnesses to this. Do take note that I'm following the dictates of Clark's feeble brain."

"So noted," Drew said, with a sharp nod.

"Hear, hear," Phil said.

"Very good," Clark said. "Now everything is under control."

"Oh, ha," Mercy said, and plunked back down in her chair.

The restaurant that Clark had selected for the business lunch with Tony Murretti was one of several mingled among the specialty shops at Stearns Wharf. An enchanting and popular attraction, the wharf had been built in 1872 to service passenger and cargo ships. The view of the harbor was lovely, as was the sight of the majestic Santa Ynez Mountains behind Santa Barbara.

Clark had purposely arrived early with Mercy in tow. He hoped their reserved table was already free, and Mercy would be safely seated before she took off her glasses.

To Clark's utmost relief, they were shown immediately to a booth overlooking the harbor. He left instructions with the hostess concerning the pending arrival of Mr. Anthony Murretti.

"Oh, what a glorious view," Mercy said, gazing out the window. "Even on a rainy day like this one, the harbor and the boats are beautiful."

"Take off your glasses," Clark said gruffly.

"Look at that cabin cruiser, Clark. Wouldn't it be something to escape from the stress of the city and spend the weekend on that?"

"Mercy, take off your glasses."

"Oh, for crying out loud." She snatched them off and shoved them into her purse. "Great. Everything is a blur. How am I supposed to read the menu?"

"I'll order for you."

"How quaint." She shook her head. "Clark, this isn't going to work. I won't be able to see Tony Murretti's face clearly enough to gauge his reaction to my presentation. This really puts me at a terrible disadvantage."

"Okay, we'll try this. If Murretti seems impressed, I'll squeeze your knee once to indicate you're to keep on that track. If I don't like the vibes he's sending out, I'll squeeze twice."

"Dumb."

"Desperate. It's all we've got. Mercy, why don't you have a spare set of contacts or an extra pair of glasses, like a normal person would?"

"Oh, but I do. My back-up glasses are in for repair, even as we speak."

Clark groaned. "I'm sorry I asked." He glanced around the large dining room, then suddenly stiffened. "Heads up, Mercy. The hostess is bringing Tony Murretti over here."

"I'm thrilled," she said dryly. "Do you think he'd be interested in playing a little anatomy by braille?"

"Shhh."

"Well, darn it, Clark, I can't see beyond my nose."

"Then look at your nose." He got to his feet and extended his hand. "Tony, how are you? I'd like you to meet my sister, Mercy Sloan."

"Miss Sloan," Tony said, after shaking Clark's hand, "it's a pleasure."

"Thank you," she said, speaking in the direction of the deep voice. "I'm delighted to meet you, Mr. Murretti."

"Please, call me Tony."

Clark sat back down on the banquette, sliding around to be close to Mercy, and Tony sat directly across from her. Clark motioned to the waitress, who appeared at their table and handed them menus. Mercy snatched one out of the air as it passed before her eyes.

This was so absurd, she thought, pretending to study the menu. She couldn't read a word unless she held the thing two inches from her nose. And all she could tell about Tony Murretti was that he was tall. Clark had said Tony was good looking, but Clark was such a dunce that she'd never take his word for it. Tony did have a deep, rich voice, a caress-you-like-velvet voice. She'd certainly like to match the face with that voice, but it wasn't going to happen today.

"Are you ready to order?" the waitress asked.

"Go ahead, Tony," Clark said.

"I'll have a steak sandwich, fries, coleslaw, and iced tea, please," Tony said.

That sounded delicious, Mercy thought. She was starving, and eager to hear what she wanted for lunch.

"The lady and I," Clark said, "will both have fresh fruit salads with cottage cheese, and a side order of wheat toast. Iced tea is fine."

"Very good," the waitress said, and lifted the menu out of Mercy's hands.

She was going to strangle Clark Sloan! Mercy fumed. She hated, and he knew she hated, cottage cheese. The rat was a dead man.

"Now then," Clark said, "to business. As I explained in your office, Tony, Mercy is in charge of custom designing the landscaping we do. She comes to the site, takes into consideration the style and size of the house, where it's located, what your prime objective is regarding the image you wish to project. Mercy?"

"What?" She blinked. "Oh! Yes. You see, Mr. Murretti—"

"Tony. It's Tony, Miss Sloan. Or may I use Mercy? It's an unusual and lovely name."

He could use little ol' Mercy for whatever he wanted to, she thought giddily. What a voice. She wouldn't be surprised if her clothes just slithered off her body. Oh, darn it, she really wished she could see his face.

"Of course . . . Tony," she said. "Please do call me Mercy."

"It's a great name, isn't it?" Clark said. "Our parents, after having three boys, decided the family was complete. When our mother told our dad there was a surprise on the way, he yelled, 'Mercy!' and that's what they named her."

Tony chuckled as Mercy wondered whether she should shoot Clark, or run him down with her car.

"As I was saying," she said, glaring in the vicinity of Clark's face. She then redirected her attention to Blur Murretti. "The first thing I need to know is your desired goal. Do you want low maintenance landscaping, or isn't that an issue because you'll be hiring a gardener? Do you want landscaping that will provide privacy? A feeling of being in the woods? Or should the grounds be unobtrusive so that attention is centered on the house itself? The possibilities are endless."

"Fascinating," Tony said. And so was Mercy Sloan, he added silently. Like her brother, she had auburn hair and brown eyes. But while Clark's good looks could be termed "rugged," Mercy's beauty was more delicate and alluring.

She was also speaking to the knot in his tie, rather than meeting his gaze. Was she shy, Miss Mercy Sloan?

"I understand from Clark," he said, "that you have a college degree in . . . I'm sorry, I've forgotten the official terminology."

"I have a bachelor's in Landscape Architecture," she said. "I'm referred to as a landscape artist, or landscape designer. So, do you have an idea of what image you wish to create with the landscaping?"

"Perfection," he said quietly. "I've waited a long time to have this house, and I designed it myself. The grounds should complement it in equal balance. Yes, I want it to be perfect."

Heavenly days, Mercy thought. The way he had said those words had sent a rush of heat swirling throughout her. *Yes, I want it to be perfect.* They were reasonable words, nothing fancy about them, but hearing him say them in his rich velvet voice, her mind had jumped the track from nice, safe landscaping to raw sensuality.

I want it to be perfect. Oh, yes, she thought dreamily, *it* would be perfect when she and Tony . . . Mercy Sloan, shame on you. Was she honestly sitting there imagining what it would be like to make love with a total stranger?

She cleared her throat. "'Perfect' might prove to be a bit subjective, but I can certainly assure you that every effort will be made to reach your expectations of—of perfection."

"I can't ask for more than that," he said.

Sure he could, she thought. He could ask for, and probably receive, whatever he wanted. Oh, drat, there she went again, thinking as crazy as a bedbug. No, no, she mustn't let the word "bed" cross her mind, even in terms of "bugs."

"Lunchtime, folks," the waitress said, startling Mercy with her sudden appearance. "Steak sandwich, fries, fruit salads . . ."

Mercy stared down at a hazy, colorful array of what she knew to be fresh fruit. But hiding in that rainbow blob was the dreaded cottage cheese. She picked up her fork and made a stab at the brightest thing she could decipher, hoping it was a cube of watermelon.

Seconds later, her taste buds exploded and her eyes widened. It was watermelon, and stuck to the bottom was a hefty dose of cottage cheese. She puffed out her cheeks and chewed as quickly as she could, swallowing the distasteful morsel.

Tony had been watching Mercy, and wondered what was wrong. She'd just resembled a chipmunk with chubby cheeks, busily chomping.

She still hadn't directly met his gaze, either. There was something strange about the lovely Miss Sloan, and it wasn't merely her behavior. He could feel an unexpected sensuality weaving between them like silken threads. How could a woman he'd just met and who refused to meet his gaze send such sparks of arousal shooting through him?

"Mercy," Clark said, interrupting Tony's thoughts. "Tony has an appointment scheduled for after lunch, so we need to proceed while we're eating. Why don't you show him the before-and-after photographs."

"Certainly," Mercy said.

What she really wanted to do was grab her glass of iced tea and take a long swallow to erase the lingering flavor of cottage cheese. But she didn't trust her depth perception. She'd probably grab Tony Murretti's glass instead.

She snapped open the briefcase she'd placed next to her on the banquette and lifted the lid. The "before" photograph was on the top, so at least there was no chance of presenting the "after" first.

"This," she said, turning the picture toward Tony, "is how the grounds of a home in Malibu looked before we started. As you can see, it's overrun with—Ow!" She jumped as Clark squeezed her leg twice, just above her knee. "Darn it, Clark, it *is* overrun with weeds."

"Oh, help," Clark muttered.

"Mercy," Tony said, "it may be overrun, but the photograph is upside down."

"It is?" She turned the picture around and squinted at it. "Oh, well, it certainly is, isn't it? It looks like weeds are growing from the sky. This probably qualifies as surreal art." She righted the picture. "There now . . . how's that?"

"Fine," Tony said, chuckling. "Those are some of the most outstanding weeds I've ever seen. But would either of you care to tell me what's going on here?"

"I give up," Clark said wearily. "Mercy, you just did your number four."

"Her what?" Tony asked.

"It's very simple, Tony," Mercy said. "I wear contact lenses, without which I can't find anything much beyond the end of my nose. I scratched a lens this morning, my back-up glasses are being repaired, and my regular glasses are, unfortunately, in the same broken boat, although I do have them with me. Clark, however, decided I'd looked like an incompetent amateur with adhesive tape holding my glasses together, so I agreed to wing it. That, obviously, was not a terrific idea."

"Oh," Tony said.

"Therefore," Mercy rushed on, rummaging in

her purse, "the glasses, complete with tape, are now leaping into action, and we can get back to business. Even more, I can avoid the cottage cheese."

"Cottage cheese?" Tony repeated, then shook his head slightly. "Never mind."

"Where in the world . . ." Mercy muttered. "Oh, here they are." She shoved the glasses on and turned to look at Tony, a bright smile on her face.

Her smile faded quickly, though, as she stared at Tony Murretti.

"Oh . . . my . . . Lord," she whispered. "You're even more gorgeous than your voice."

"Mercy," Clark hissed. He glanced at Tony, then at Mercy, then back to Tony. "She didn't say that. I mean, she said it, but she was joking. She has a great sense of humor, doesn't she? Funny little Mercy Sloan, that's my sister." He glared at said sister. "You wouldn't really say that to one of our most important prospective clients, would you, Mercy? No, of course not. Mercy? Are you listening to me?"

She was not. She was too busy cataloging every feature of Tony Murretti's face. She'd never seen such dark, dark eyes, and they were framed by lashes that matched the night blackness of his thick hair. He was so devastatingly handsome, with well-defined cheekbones, a square chin, a wonderfully Roman nose, his face might have been sculpted by Michelangelo.

His Italian heritage gave his skin a natural olive hue, and his lips seemed to be calling to her to taste and feel them with her own.

Tony Murretti, Mercy thought, was the most marvelously magnificent masculine man that she had ever seen. Her heart was beating crazily, and that heat she'd felt before had ceased swirling and was now pounding.

"Mercy!" Clark said.

She nearly leapt off the banquette in shock at his outburst. "What! Oh, right, I know what you want, Clark. Here we go. We've done the 'before' picture so"—she reached into her briefcase—"we move right along to the 'after.' There you are, Tony, and lo and behold, it's even right side up."

Tony had to force himself to switch his gaze from Mercy to the picture. Mercy Sloan was obviously an intelligent woman, and judging even from just one photograph, she was an extremely talented landscape artist. A woman, he mused, who loved the outdoors, sunshine and fresh air and things that grow.

Mercy Sloan would be a wonderful companion for the right man. He was not, however, that man.

"I'm very impressed," he said, pulling himself back to the subject at hand. "If it weren't for the house, I'd never have known those two photographs were of the same lot. I'd like to have you see my place, give me some ideas on what you visualize there. If I agree with your choices, I'll be ready to sign a contract."

"Excellent," Clark said.

"I prefer to be able to view the area from inside the house as well as outside," Mercy said. "Would that be possible during the day?"

Tony smiled. "I'm the boss of Murretti Investments. If I'm late to work, I won't fire myself. Could you be at the house tomorrow morning at nine o'clock? Clark has the address."

"That will be fine," Mercy said.

He nodded. "Good." For the moment, he thought, everything was perfect.

Two

The next morning, Tony stood at the floor-to-ceiling windows in the front of his living room, gazing out over the rolling foothills and the majestic mountains in the distance. The rain had stopped the previous evening, leaving the air clear and fresh, and everything appearing sparkling clean. He held a large ceramic mug in one hand, and periodically took swallows of the strong, rich coffee it contained.

Turning slowly, he swept his gaze over the enormous living room. Large comfortable furniture in tones of beige and brown, with accent colors of orange and yellow, sat about the room. The carpet was dun colored, reminding him of a sandy beach, and a flagstone fireplace covered nearly half of the far wall.

Bookshelves climbed to the ceiling on both sides of the fireplace, the shelves holding a multitude of books as well as carefully selected *objets d'art*. The shelves, tables, and wood trim on the furniture were all natural oak, enhancing the sense of the outdoors having been brought inside.

"Perfect," Tony said aloud.

The entire house was perfect. The huge kitchen, the bathrooms, his meticulously planned office, the five bedrooms upstairs, all of it had been designed by him. After the house was built, he'd interviewed several decorators, then had worked closely with the one he hired, sparing no expense.

The result was perfection, but Tony wouldn't have settled for less.

He turned again to look out of the windows.

Now, the landscaping. Again, he'd interviewed many people, choosing at last Sloan Nursery and Landscaping. He'd liked their enthusiasm, attitude, and approach, the concept that the house and grounds should be in concert with each other.

And he liked Mercy Sloan.

Tony frowned, then drained his mug. Where had that thought come from. *He liked Mercy Sloan.* Well, yes, he liked her. So what? She was attractive, confident, looked directly at him when she spoke . . .

He chuckled, then mentally corrected himself. Mercy looked directly at him, when she was able to see him. The glasses she'd finally put on had been ridiculous with the lump of tape as their main attraction. But for some reason, the adhesive-taped frames had added to Mercy's rather endearing personality.

Endearing and puzzling, he mused. Although she was an obviously competent landscape artist, he'd felt an odd urge to protect her.

He couldn't recall ever feeling particularly protective about the women he dated. They were all self-sufficient and career oriented, and they made it clear from the onset that they could hold their own in a male-centered business world. They wanted to be accepted, not protected, and woe to the man who tried a knight-in-shining armor approach with them.

But Mercy wasn't like that, which made him wonder at the familiar heat of desire he'd felt when he'd first seen her. He didn't want a woman in his life who would expect him to give more than the bare minimum of himself. And Mercy Sloan was definitely that kind of woman.

He strode into the kitchen and put his mug in the dishwasher. As he wandered back into the living room, he saw a small blue car coming up the winding driveway.

A minute later, Mercy got out of the car with briefcase in hand and glanced around.

Oh, hell, Tony thought as his body instantly reacted to the sight of her. He could hear the wild thump of his heart echoing in his ears, and feel the ache of passion low and deep within him.

This was ridiculous, he admonished himself. Mercy Sloan looked like a kid standing out there. She was wearing jeans, red tennis shoes, and a short-sleeved red top. The top should have clashed harshly with her hair, but it didn't. No, it was great, the way it outlined her small breasts . . .

Jeans and tennis shoes were not a turn-on, he told himself firmly. Well, yes, those jeans fit her like a second skin, and she had a nice little bottom, and sweetly curving hips, and long legs . . .

Knock it off! She was walking toward his front door, and if he didn't stop this insane inner dialogue with himself, he was going to embarrass both of them.

He crossed the wide entryway and opened the door just as Mercy raised one hand with the forefinger extended to press the bell.

Neither spoke, nor moved, nor hardly breathed. They simply stood there, gazes locked. Time became inconsequential as they stared at each other and drifted into a hazy, sensual world.

Mercy told herself to move, to blink, to say something, but she couldn't. Tony had enraptured her.

She'd dreamed of him throughout the night, then thought of him when she first awakened.

As she'd driven to his home, she'd tried to convince herself that her mental picture of Tony Murretti depicted him as far more magnificent than he actually was.

But that was not the case. He was everything . . . no, heaven help her, he was even *more* than she'd envisioned him to be.

A fluttering in her stomach swelled into a whirlpool of sensations, gathering heat as it rushed through her, leaving a trail of fiery desire in its wake. Her breasts felt unusually sensitive, needing a soothing touch that she somehow knew only Tony could provide.

Good Lord, she thought, with a sudden flash of panic, what was happening to her? What was Tony Murretti doing to her?

With every ounce of willpower she possessed, she tore her gaze from his and stared instead at her finger, still poised to ring the doorbell. She dropped her hand quickly to her side.

"Lovely house," she said to his chest. "The design is crisp and clean, yet it carries out the Spanish motif of the area. The red-tile roof and white exterior are striking. And it certainly is a large house. But you're a large man, so that makes sense, I guess. The view from here is certainly—"

"Mercy."

"—sensational. Everything is so fresh and pretty from the rain, and—"

"Mercy, look at me."

She halted her monologue. "I am."

"No, you're not. You're talking to my shirt."

Wrong, she thought. The heck with the shirt. She was directing her blather to the man's *chest*, even going so far as to wonder what said chest would look like without the shirt.

It would be a beautiful chest, of that she was certain. Covered with curly hair as dark as that on his gorgeous head, his chest would be tautly muscled and perfectly proportioned to his arms. The arms that would reach for her, gather her close, then . . .

"Mercy."

"What!"

"Did I wake you?" he asked dryly. He stepped back. "Would you care to come in?"

She nodded curtly, then marched past him. She was getting her act together that very second, she told herself. She was behaving like a silly adolescent in the throes of her first crush. What was next on her idiotic agenda? She'd fling herself into Tony Murretti's arms and say, "Take me, I'm yours"? Enough, Mercy Sloan, was enough.

She stopped and turned to face him. "I really like the parquet floor in this entryway," she said to his chin.

Tony planted his hands on his knees and bent over, bringing his eyes directly in line with hers.

"You've progressed from my shirt to my chin,"

he said, "but that still leaves a conversation with my nose before you actually look at me. Or can't you see me clearly?"

"Oh, yes, I can see you. I went to the optometrist this morning before I drove up here, and he was able to buff the scratch out of my contact lens."

"Good. I'm going to straighten up now, Mercy, because I'm already getting a kink in my back. You keep your eyes looking at my eyes, okay?"

"I don't think that's a terrific idea."

He slowly straightened, and against her better judgment, her gaze remained locked with his.

"Why isn't looking at me a terrific idea?" he asked. "Because you felt what I did when I opened the door? You did feel it, didn't you? That same desire we felt yesterday, growing stronger and stronger? How long did we stand there, Mercy? I don't know. Do you?"

"Tony," she whispered, "don't."

"I'm only asking for answers to reasonable questions, Mercy. Something strange happens every time we look at each other. You can't deny that. I want to know what it is."

"Well, how in the blue blazes should *I* know?" she exclaimed, her voice rising. "Nothing like that ever happened to me before. I'm not in the habit of being unable to move, just because some big lummox is hypnotizing me, or whatever, with the darkest, most mesmerizing eyes

I've ever seen. And I usually don't fantasize about what it would be like to . . . to . . ."

Her voice trailed off, and a warm flush of embarrassment stained her cheeks. She whipped one hand back and forth in the air.

"Erase all that. Those words were never spoken. I didn't say them, so you didn't hear them."

Tony spread his legs slightly and folded his arms over his chest. He studied her, a thoughtful expression on his face.

"Would you stop that?" she yelled. "You cheat, do you know that? Look at you. There you stand in a pose that is so incredibly male, you obviously expect me to throw myself at your feet. Don't try to get tricky with me, Murretti. I wasn't born yesterday, you know."

"You're yelling at me," he said incredulously, "because of the way I'm standing in my own entryway?"

Mercy opened her mouth to retort, then thought better of it.

"Oh," she said quietly. "When you put it like that, it sounds absurd. I think we should pretend that I just arrived, and you're about to give me a tour of the house. Okay?"

"No."

"Why not?"

"Because . . . Oh, hell, forget it." He strode past her. "The living room is here on the left."

"I need to take notes," she said, following him.

And he needed his head examined, Tony thought as he entered the large, sunny room. Why had he asked her those questions? What difference did it make that he'd never experienced such intense and instantaneous reactions to a woman before? It was a fluke, an unexplainable occurrence that should be ignored, not explored.

He was not now, nor was he ever going to be, interested in a serious, committed relationship with a woman. He didn't want to hear any declarations of love, any promises to stay with him for all time.

So, no, he really didn't want to know what sort of magic Mercy worked on him.

Magic? his mind echoed. Where had that word come from? He was a realist, a man who dealt only in facts. Magic was whimsical, elusive. There was no room for magic in his world. There was no room for Mercy Sloan.

"I have the notes I need for this room," Mercy said, bringing Tony from his reverie.

"What? Oh, all right." He hadn't realized she'd been writing on a yellow legal pad. "Do you want to see the view from the kitchen windows?"

"Yes, please. I'll do this as quickly as possible. I imagine you must be eager to get to your office."

"There's no rush," he said. "Take your time." Why the hell had he said that? He had a mountain of work on his desk at the office, telephone calls to make, people to see. He should be hustling Mercy out of there so he could get into town. "Come on," he said gruffly. "The kitchen is this way, in the back of the house."

As Tony strode across the room, Mercy followed, her gaze sliding over him.

He was wearing steel-gray trousers and a pale blue dress shirt open at the neck. His shoulders looked a block wide, his hips were narrow, and his legs were obviously nicely muscled. She couldn't complain about the enticing condition of his tush, either.

What was silly, she admitted, was the feeling that she was seeing him in an intimate situation, since he wasn't wearing a tie and suit coat. It was as though he were only half-dressed. What a dangerously provocative thought.

Warning herself once more to get her mind on track, Mercy entered the kitchen. She made the appropriate complimentary comments about the size and lovely decor, while her mind blithely skittered back to what had taken place when Tony had first opened the door. The sensations she'd experienced had been so disturbing, yet also exciting. She'd felt an incredible heat, and a desire more intense than anything she'd ever known before.

What did it mean? Why had it happened? Tony had demanded answers from her, then he'd suddenly pulled back, dismissing the incident with an irate "Forget it."

Did *she* want those answers? Mercy asked herself. Did she need to know what her reactions to Tony Murretti meant? Yes. If it was simply physical, lust in its purest form, she'd scold herself in self-disgust and go about her business.

But what if emotions were involved? Especially considering Tony's forceful "Forget it."

She stifled a sigh, amazed that her life had suddenly gotten so complicated. If meeting Tony Murretti was the first of one of her ever-famous series of four, would it be a good four, or bad? Shouldn't she at least know the answer to *that* question?

She made several more notes on her pad, then turned to look at Tony. He was leaning against a counter, his arms loosely folded across his chest, one foot crossed over the other.

It was, she thought wearily, another one of those ultramasculine poses that he struck naturally, with no conscious ploy to seduce. He was one-hundred-percent male, no doubt about it.

"That's all I need inside the house," she said.

"Oh? You don't want to see the view from the bedrooms upstairs?"

"No, it won't be necessary to go to the bedrooms."

He smiled. It was a very slow, very male smile, and he accompanied it with a slight nod.

"Interesting," he said.

Mercy fought the strong urge to slug him.

"Therefore," she went on, hoping her voice had a ring of authoritativeness to it, "I'll be going outside now. The property-line stakes are still up and flagged, so I'll be able to look over the whole area. I'll need to take soil samples too."

"Why?"

"I always do. I don't anticipate any problems, but I prefer to be certain. I'll have the county agricultural department run tests for acidity. As far as I know, all the soil in this area is in excellent balance, so I don't think we'll need any large additions of mulch."

"You're very efficient."

"Yes, I am."

He chuckled. "And modest."

"I'm good at what I do, Tony."

He met her gaze directly, and his smile faded.

"So am I, Mercy."

Mercy couldn't move. She felt as though her tennis shoes were stuck to the floor with Super Glue. She had the distinct impression that somewhere in this banal conversation they'd shifted from talking about landscaping and investments. There was a definite undercurrent of sex in the air.

Get out of there, Mercy told herself. The

ground she was suddenly treading on was much too dangerous. She had to get out of that house, and put some distance between herself and Tony.

"So!" she said much too loudly. She started across the room, very aware that she had to pass Tony to make her escape. "I'll finish up outside, but there's no reason why you can't go on to your office."

She was three steps beyond him before he spoke.

"Mercy."

She stopped. It was as though the sound of her name spoken in that deep, velvety voice had pushed a button that halted her flight. She kept her back to him, but she could feel his heated gaze rake down her spine, sending shivers in its wake.

"Yes?" she whispered.

Don't do it, Murretti, Tony told himself. *Let her go.*

He pushed himself away from the counter and moved to stand in front of her. Slowly, he lifted his hands to frame her face, then tilted her head back to meet his gaze.

So soft, he thought. Her cheeks were so soft, just as he knew her lips would be when he kissed her.

No, Murretti. Don't do it.

"Mercy," he said, his voice rough with rising passion, "about the landscaping . . . I want . . .

From where I can see it out the front window, I want . . . a Christmas tree. Could you do that, Mercy? Plant a Christmas tree where I can see it every day? That would be perfect, if you could."

"Yes," she said, her eyes never looking away from his. "I'll find you the most beautiful Christmas tree you've ever seen. Is there . . . is there anything else that you want?"

"Yes," he murmured, and his mouth melted over hers.

For just a moment, Mercy wondered about Christmas trees. There'd been such yearning in Tony's voice when he'd asked for the tree, such a vulnerable, raw expression on his face before he swept the emotions away.

But then rational thought fled as Tony parted her lips and his tongue delved into the sweet darkness of her mouth. She nestled closer to him, savoring his strength, his warmth, the feel of his arousal pressing against her.

She wanted this man, she thought hazily. She wanted to make love with Tony Murretti, to give all of herself to him. Never had such want and need consumed her, like a wildfire raging out of control.

She'd always been cautious in her relationships with men, but not this time. Because this was Tony, and this was the best thing that had ever happened to her.

Tony lifted his head only far enough to draw a ragged breath, then captured Mercy's mouth once more, plummeting his tongue deep within. His body screamed for release, aching to join with Mercy's, to fill her, to give and take and be one entity in ecstasy.

But it was more than just physical, he realized in some still coherent section of his mind. Emotions were rising within him, too, foreign emotions that he could not name, emotions that terrified him.

Lord, what was happening to him? What was Mercy Sloan doing to him? He was out of control, slipping toward the edge of an abyss he had no intention of falling into. He had to stop kissing Mercy Sloan now, separate himself from her and regain command of his emotions.

Now!

He tore his mouth from hers and gripped her shoulders with shaking hands. As he inched her away from himself, he instantly missed the feel of her body nestling so close.

He stifled a groan as he gazed at her parted lips, moist from his kisses, beckoning for more. She slowly raised her lashes, and he saw in her brown eyes the desire that mirrored his own.

Mustering willpower from a source unknown, he dropped his hands from her shoulders and stepped back.

"That," he said, his voice harsh from thwarted passion, "shouldn't have happened."

"Why not?" she asked, her own voice breathless. "Are you sorry that you kissed me, Tony? Is that what you're saying?"

"Yes." He dragged a hand through his hair. "I mean, no." He shook his head. "Hell, let it go, Mercy. Forget that I . . . that we . . . Just forget what took place here."

"No, I refuse to do that," she said, lifting her chin. "You can dismiss it from your mind if you wish, but I have the right to do whatever I please with my memories."

She crossed her arms firmly over her breasts and raised her chin another inch.

"I'm keeping the memory of those kisses, thank you very much." She paused, then a bubble of laughter escaped from her lips. "So there," she added. "I sound about four years old. I'll probably stamp my foot any second now."

Tony smiled despite himself. Her laughter, the sparkle in her eyes, were infectious.

"You are something, Mercy Sloan," he said. "You must drive your brothers crazy trying to keep you out of harm's way."

"I don't need their watchdog tactics."

"You need a keeper, I think." His smile slowly faded, and was replaced by a frown. "Mercy, I'm the kind of guy your brothers would definitely warn you to stay away from."

"Oh? Are you a rotten person?"

"Let's just say I live in a different world from you. You come from a close-knit family, surrounded by people who care about you, love you. I learned as I was researching landscaping companies that the Sloans are fiercely loyal to one another."

"And?"

"And I'm a loner. I live completely alone, answering to no one, being accountable only to myself. I strive for perfection in everything I do, and ask the maximum of those around me. I have no time, Mercy, nor the desire, to settle down anywhere, to commit myself to one person. It's obvious that you're family oriented. You want a husband, children, a home like the one you were raised in."

"Is all this great information tattooed on my forehead?" she asked, frowning.

"Can you deny that it's true?"

"Well, no, but . . ."

"Mercy, I learned very early in life to size people up correctly on the first go, because there isn't room for error. I've had a lot of years of experience doing it, and I don't make mistakes. Everything about you brings up images of babies and flower gardens and brownies fresh from the oven. Now do you understand why what happened between us is best forgotten?"

"Wait," Mercy said, raising one hand. "Back up here a bit. You said you have no desire to settle down anywhere. If that's the case, then why did you build this house? Why are you living here? I can't believe it was an investment for resale purposes. That doesn't work, Tony, because of the Christmas tree."

Anger flashed across his face, shining in the obsidian depths of his eyes. Mercy forced herself to keep her gaze riveted on his, telling herself that she would *not* be the one to first look away.

Silence hung heavily in the air. Seconds ticked by as Tony strove to rein in his anger.

Finally, he drew in a deep breath and let it out slowly. "You," he said, pointing one long finger at her, "are driving me crazy."

He spun on his heel and strode out of the kitchen.

"Well, that was a rude thing to say," Mercy muttered.

But then again, she pondered, tapping a fingertip against her chin, one must be getting to someone a tad if that someone has said he's going crazy. It certainly made sense to her.

Tony Murretti was one complicated man. He'd allow her only brief, confusing glimpses of who he really was, then he would slide a solid barrier into place.

One thing was certain, though. She was keeping the memories of Tony's kisses tucked away in a private, safe place in her heart.

Three

Sitting on a high wooden stool in front of a drafting table, Mercy stared absently out the large side window of Sloan Nursery and Landscaping.

She was vaguely aware that it was a beautiful day. The May sun was warm, the sky a brilliant blue with fluffy white clouds decorating the heavens like whipped cream on a splendid cake.

Customers had been streaming into the nursery the entire morning, keeping her brothers busy. The citizens of Santa Barbara were eager to begin planting their vegetable and flower gardens, and to reseed and fertilize their lawns.

Business was booming, Mercy thought idly. Her now retired parents would be pleased with the accountant's report when they returned from the cruise they were on. That cruise had been a dream of theirs for years.

Mercy frowned, finally realizing how much her thoughts were drifting. And she knew why she couldn't concentrate on anything. It was all Tony Murretti's fault.

She plunked her elbows on the drafting table and rested her chin in her hands. It hardly seemed possible that she'd met Tony a mere five days before. It was as though he'd occupied her mind for an extremely long time.

But, no. They'd had lunch on Monday, she'd been to his house on Tuesday, she'd worked on the plans for his property on Wednesday and Thursday, and there she sat on Friday, a befuddled creature who couldn't get the man off her mind.

She was certain now that meeting Tony had been number one of a pending series of four marvelous events. Number two had been the kisses shared with him in his kitchen. What part of her psyche had voted on the good versus the bad designation, she had no idea.

All she really knew was that during the days and on into her dreams at night, the image, the memories of Tony, were pushing aside every other issue in her life.

"Oh, Mercy, you're acting so ridiculous," she said aloud. She had to get a handle on her infatuation, regain control of her total being. If her brothers weren't so busy, they would have already picked up on the fact that she was behaving like a moonstruck adolescent. And if they learned *why* she was behaving this way, they'd lock her in her room for a year.

The door to the office opened and Phil entered, snapping Mercy out of her reverie.

"Hi, kid," he said, not looking at her as he strode to his desk. "How's it going? Are you about ready to set up a meeting with Tony Murretti to present your plans?"

"I . . ."

"Where's the invoice for the decorative bark we ordered? We're running low, and I need to know when to expect delivery." He shuffled through some papers on his desk. "Okay, here we go. Good. It's due tomorrow. No problem." He turned to look at Mercy. "So?"

"So?" she said, smiling brightly. "Well, isn't that nice that the decorative bark is expected here tomorrow? There's nothing more annoying than being out of decorative bark. It is a vitally important—"

"Halt," Phil said, slicing one hand through the air. "Spill it, Mercy. You've been acting weird all week. What's going on with you?"

"You're imagining things, Phil. You haven't had time to notice that I'm acting weird. What I mean is, I'm *not* acting weird. I'm in a mind-set of high concentration, a genius-level production mode. Tony Murretti is really into 'perfect,' and if I don't create 'perfect,' we run the risk of not getting his big-bucks contract. Because you're a dumb-dumb, you don't realize how the mind of a genius works. But that's all right, because we genius types are very tolerant of less gifted mortals. Good-bye, Phil. I'm extremely busy."

"Not bad," he said, nodding. "That was one of your finer phony spiels. Now that we've gotten that baloney out of the way, you can tell me why you're acting weird. Hey, baby sister, this is me, Phil, remember? You can't snow me, but you can trust me. What's wrong?"

She sighed. "Tony Murretti."

"The plans for landscaping his property aren't going well?"

"I had no difficulties at all with the plans. I'll have the colored drawing ready for presentation to him in about an hour."

Phil glanced at the large paper tacked onto the drafting board, then redirected his attention to Mercy, confusion evident on his face.

"The drawing looks great, Mercy. You've definitely lost me, though. You said you're acting weird because of Tony Murretti and . . ." He stopped speaking and raised his eyebrows. "Ah. The light dawns. It's Tony Murretti, the man, who has you in a dither, not his property."

"Yes," she said miserably. "Phil, promise me you won't say anything to Clark and Drew. I just couldn't handle their inquisition right now. In fact, I don't want a zillion questions from you, either. I know you love me and only want to help, but I just need to be left alone so I can hopefully sort things through."

"Sometimes things become clearer when you explain them to another person, Mercy. You know, get it out where you can look at it."

She shook her head.

"Well, I'm here if you decide you want to talk about it." He paused. "Mercy, Clark said that Murretti is too . . . well, too experienced for you. I hope you're not forgetting that."

"No, I'm not forgetting it," she said, turning her head to look at the drawing.

Nor was she forgetting that the "too experienced" tough-guy Murretti wanted a Christmas tree in his yard where he could always see it.

And she was not forgetting the pain and vulnerability she'd glimpsed in Tony when he'd asked her for a Christmas tree. There were depths to him that she was sure he revealed to no one, and she was equally sure that his slipup with her had been the cause of his anger.

Oh, he was an enigma, that Tony Murretti. Cancel her declaration of being a genius. If she had even half a brain, she'd plunk Tony into a "strictly business" slot, and that would be that. But her *entire* brain must be on vacation, because she knew she couldn't just walk away from him. Not yet, not yet.

"Mercy?" Phil said.

She forced a smile. "Don't fret about me, Phil.

You should be thinking about your very pregnant wife. Julie needs a lot of tender loving care these days, you know. I'm fine, really I am."

"Well," he said, "if you should get to be 'not fine,' I'll be here." He kissed her on the forehead. "I love ya, kid."

"And I love you, even if you are a fussbudget. Now, shoo, go away. I want to finish this drawing, then call and find out if there's any chance of getting an appointment with Tony this afternoon."

"Okay, I'll leave you to it. But, Mercy . . . Be careful. If Murretti breaks your heart, I'll feel obligated to punch him out, and I'm getting too old for that stuff."

She laughed. "I'll keep that in mind."

After Phil left the office, Mercy frowned at the drawing.

If Murretti breaks your heart . . . What a dismal thought. But the cold trickle of fear inside her warned her that Tony Murretti might very well do just that.

Tony swore under his breath, then began to read the detailed report from the first line . . . again.

"Hell," he said a minute later, and tossed the folder onto his desk.

He laced his fingers behind his neck and

leaned back in his leather chair, scowling at the ceiling.

He couldn't concentrate, and it was all Mercy Sloan's fault. And he was not one bit happy about it. From the moment he'd driven away from his house on Tuesday, leaving her tromping through the weeds in her red tennis shoes, she'd occupied front row center in his mind.

This wasn't like him. But then, he reasoned, he'd never met anyone like Mercy Sloan before. That, however, was no excuse. It didn't explain why she was consuming his brain, and causing his body to ache with fiery want at the mere thought of her.

Dammit, Mercy wasn't even his type. He'd told her that in no uncertain terms, right there in the middle of his kitchen.

What he'd said was true. He knew it, Mercy knew it, but for some insane and extremely annoying reason, his mind and body were totally ignoring his sound reasoning.

The intercom on his phone buzzed. He leaned forward and pressed the button.

"Yes, Marianne?"

"I have Mercy Sloan on hold, Tony. She'd like to see you this afternoon to present the landscaping plans for your house. You're free at four o'clock. Shall I tell her to come then?"

"I . . . No, make it five o'clock."

"Five? That's quitting time."

"You can leave at five, but tell Mercy that's all I have open on my schedule."

"Okay."

"Let me know what she says."

"Sure thing, boss."

Tony released the button and groaned. He was, he decided, certifiably nuts. Why hadn't he told Marianne to tell Mercy to come at four? By five at the latest, he would have been shuffling Mercy out the door, and everything would have been under control.

But that would have been the intelligent course of action, he thought dryly, and when it came to Mercy, he obviously preferred to act like an idiotic jerk. Kissing her, for example. That definitely had been idiotic.

Instantly, Tony knew he was lying to himself. Kissing her had been fabulous. She'd felt wonderful pressed against him, had tasted like sweet honey and smelled like wildflowers. Those kisses had ignited a fire within him he'd been unable to quell.

Control, Murretti, he directed himself. He'd set up a potentially dangerous situation by scheduling Mercy's appointment for after regular working hours, but he'd deal with it just fine. With any luck, she would refuse to come that late, and wait until next week.

The intercom buzzed, and he quickly pressed the button.

"Speak, Marianne," he said.

"Mercy Sloan will be here at five."

"Thank you." So much for luck. Control was the optimum word. He had a business appointment at five o'clock regarding the landscaping to be done at his home, and he would conduct himself accordingly. Everything was under control.

At five minutes before five o'clock, Mercy entered the reception area of Murretti Investments. She glanced quickly around, silently approving of the southwestern theme that had been used in the decor.

A large desk sat at one end of the area, a woman seated behind it. She stood as Mercy walked toward her.

"You must be Mercy Sloan," the woman said, smiling at her. "I'm Marianne, Tony's administrative assistant."

Tony's *gorgeous* administrative assistant, Mercy mentally corrected. Marianne was tall and willowy, and had short, curly blond hair and a sensational figure. She appeared to be in her late twenties, and was so beautiful, it was disgusting.

"Yes, I'm Mercy Sloan," she said, hoping her smile looked at least semigenuine.

"I'll let Tony know you've arrived, then I'm going to scoot out of here. I have a dinner date with my husband which is going to cost him a bundle because I'm famished. I'll be back in a jiffy." She turned and disappeared down a corridor.

Husband? Mercy thought. Marvelous Marianne had a husband? Well, wasn't that nice?

Realizing that she was edging toward hysteria, Mercy cleared his throat, lifted her chin, and straightened her shoulders. The day had crept by like a sluggish turtle, and the closer it came to five o'clock, the more nervous she had become.

Which was, she told herself, really ridiculous. After all, it wasn't as though she was about to meet a famous movie star for the first time. This was only Tony Murretti.

Only Tony Murretti? A snide little voice in her mind echoed. The Tony Murretti who had done tricky things to her heart and body from the moment she'd seen him. No, correct that. From the moment she'd heard his voice.

The Tony Murretti who had kissed her senseless in his kitchen, evoking within her a potent desire she had not known she possessed.

The Tony Murretti who had depths she yearned to explore, discovering the real and total man behind his barriers. Tony, who wanted a Christmas tree.

That was who she was there to see. And the realization that she was only seconds away from that encounter sent her heart racing and her knees trembling.

Strictly business, Mercy, she reminded herself. Leaping into Tony's arms would not be considered a classy move. She was aiming for sophistication and professionalism here, a cool and collected presentation of her excellent plans for his landscaping.

Okay, she thought, she was ready. Bring on Magnificent Murretti. She could handle this. Strictly business.

"Miss Sloan?"

"Who? Oh! Yes?"

"Tony will see you now," Marianne said. She took her purse out of the bottom drawer of her desk. "His office is down at the end of the hall. Have a lovely evening. Good night."

"'Night," Mercy mumbled as Marianne left the reception area. The door closed behind her with a soft click.

Mercy didn't move. She stood motionless in the silence, the only sound being the echo of her own heartbeat in her ears.

She wanted to go home, she thought. She'd crawl into bed, pull the blankets over her head, and not emerge until she was eighty-two and too old to be thrown for a loop by an incredibly handsome man who kissed like a dream.

"Oh, shut up, Mercy," she said, and started down the hallway.

When she completed her trek, which she figured had been three miles long, she stopped at the open doorway of Tony's office. Her gaze swept over the huge room. A wall of glistening windows allowed a fantastic view of Santa Barbara, eight floors below. Hanging on the other walls were the impressive oil paintings of Italy that Clark had spoken of. On the right side of the room were a sofa and two easy chairs set around a round table.

Having noted everything else in the room, Mercy finally shifted her gaze to the gleaming mahogany desk with a dark leather top.

There was Tony Murretti.

And he was looking directly at her, his face expressionless.

He wasn't wearing his jacket, and he'd folded back his shirtsleeves, revealing muscular forearms covered in a smattering of dark hair. His tie was pulled down several inches, and the top button of his pale green shirt was undone. His hair, his thick, luscious dark hair, was tousled, as though he'd restlessly dragged his fingers through it. He was just a bit disheveled and tired looking, and Mercy thought he was the most beautiful thing she had ever seen.

He got to his feet. "Hello, Mercy. Come in." He swept one arm in the general direction of the two chairs in front of his desk. "Have a seat."

Oh, feet, Mercy begged silently, please move. She only had to cover an acre or two of space before she'd be able to sink gratefully into one of those chairs.

She took a deep breath and crossed the room.

When she plunked down in one of the chairs, she inwardly cheered that her wobbly legs had accomplished their goal.

Tony resumed his seat in his leather chair. He propped his elbows on the arms and made a steeple of his fingers, touching the tips to his lips.

Five o'clock, he thought wryly, and all was definitely not well. Heat was coiling deep within him as his body tautened with arousal. His heart was beating hard and fast, and it was all he could do to keep from leaping over the desk and hauling Mercy into his arms.

Mercy Sloan, with her tumble of auburn curls, her big brown eyes, her delicate features and enticing lips, was turning him inside out. She was like fresh spring air and warm sunshine, and he smiled inwardly as he thought of how well her brightly flowered skirt suited her. She had a smile that lit up her face and caused her eyes to sparkle, and her laughter reminded him of delightful tinkling bells. She was completely different from all the other women he knew, and from himself.

Yet he wanted her.

He dropped his hands and cleared his throat, pushing his wandering, sensual thoughts to a dusty corner of his mind. Leaning forward, he loosely linked his fingers on the top of the desk.

"How have you been?" he asked, his voice not

as smooth and controlled as he would have liked.

"Fine. Busy. I have a plan to present to you for the landscaping."

"All right."

She snapped open her briefcase and removed a matted drawing. She set it on his desk.

"This is a rendering of what I propose for your property. You understand, of course, that you can reject any part of it that isn't to your liking. I'll redo it as many times as necessary until it is, in your opinion, perfect."

He nodded.

"I'll explain to you what each of these selections are, and why I chose them."

"Wouldn't it be easier if we were both looking at it from the same side?" he asked. "You'll have to view it upside down from there."

"Oh, upside down is no problem," Mercy said quickly. No way, she thought. She was *not* getting elbow-to-elbow cozy with this man. "Now then, the—"

Tony stood up. "This really isn't efficient, Mercy." He picked up the drawing and walked out from behind his desk.

Oh, help, she thought, her eyes widening as he approached her. Go away, Tony Murretti. Shoo. Scat. Do *not* sit down in that chair.

Tony pushed the other chair over to hers until the arms bumped, then sat down.

"There," he said, "that's much better." Actually, he thought, it constituted torture. Why had he done this? Why hadn't he stayed safely behind his desk, and let Mercy stand on her head to explain the landscaping if need be? Now she was only inches away, and he wanted so badly to pull her onto his lap and . . . "Proceed," he said. "I mean, tell me what I'm looking at in this drawing. It's all very attractive, by the way."

He had rude thighs, Mercy thought, swallowing the strange giggle that threatened to escape from her lips. His thighs strained against the expensive material of his slacks, clearly defining the taut muscles beneath. Very rude.

His after-shave smelled exceptionally good, too, and that wasn't very considerate, either. He was so big, and so male, and so there, and she'd never seen those stupid plants in that picture before in her life.

"Mercy?"

"Hmmm?" She looked up at him, wondering why she couldn't quite focus on him. "Yes, Tony?"

"Oh, yes, Mercy," he said, his voice deep and rumbly.

He lowered his head toward hers . . . closer, closer . . . anticipating the moment when his mouth would capture hers, his tongue would delve between her lips, and he'd drink the nectar of her sweet taste.

Mercy suddenly stiffened. "Deciduous trees," she said.

Tony stared at her for a long moment.

"What?" he asked.

"Across the back of your property," she said, forcing herself to look at the drawing he held. "See? Those are all from the deciduous group. They'll provide shade and privacy, and will act as a wind barrier. They're graceful, lovely, and grow quickly."

He directed his attention to the drawing, too. "Oh."

"I've shown maples there," she rushed on. "Amur, Japanese, Norway, sugar, rock, scarlet maples. The list of choices goes on and on, but they'll all do splendidly."

"Oh."

"Lining the driveway would be lilac bushes. They grow beautifully this close to water, and I'd prefer to go with white blossoms, rather than blue or lavender. White would complement the house. Lilacs make a marvelous natural border, and smell heavenly."

"Oh. That's nice."

"And there, in the front, is your Christmas tree. I gave it a great deal of thought and decided on a fir tree, instead of a pine. There are many species of fir—balsam, Douglas, et cetera. I've settled on—providing you approve, of course— a white fir. It has bluish-green needles, plus cones. I have a twelve foot one on hold for you, which would eventually grow to anywhere from thirty to fifty feet. It will be sturdy and—"

"Mercy."

She slowly turned her head to meet his gaze. "—a perfect—"

"I need to kiss you now, Mercy."

"—Christmas tree that you—"

"Now."

"—can enjoy for years and . . . Oh, yes, Tony, kiss me before I faint."

He slid one hand to the nape of her neck and urged her closer as he bent toward her. His mouth melted over hers in a searing kiss that she returned with equal hunger. Their tongues met in the darkness of her mouth, and passions soared.

A groan rumbled in Tony's chest. A sigh of pleasure purred in Mercy's throat. Both were consumed by a pulsing heat that swept through them, spreading flames of desire. All thoughts of landscaping and Christmas trees vanished. They knew only want and need.

With quick, smooth motions—and without breaking the kiss—Tony slid the drawing onto his desk, gripped Mercy's shoulders, and urged her to stand with him. He encircled her with his arms and pulled her body tight against his.

Mercy's arms floated upward to entwine around his neck. Her breasts were crushed to his hard chest, and she nearly cried her need for him to soothe them with his fingers and his tongue. The rhythmic duel and dance of their tongues was matched by a surge of hot blood low and deep within her.

Tony's hands boldly slipped beneath her sweater, gliding upward across the soft skin of her back. Easing away from her slightly, he allowed his hands to slide around to the sides of her breasts. She tensed, waiting. When his thumbs stroked her nipples, hardening them instantly, she moaned into his mouth and pressed her hips tightly against his.

Tony nearly lost it. His entire body ached, burned, with the need to make Mercy Sloan his.

"I want you," he said, his lips still against hers. He hardly recognized his own voice, it was so rough with passion. "Lord, I want you so damn much."

"Yes, yes, I want . . . I want you too. I really . . . Oh, Tony."

The honesty and bewilderment in her voice pierced through his single-minded need. What are you doing? he yelled at himself. This was Mercy Sloan, he was seducing, a woman he couldn't have because she needed more than he could ever give. Dear God, he had to get himself under control.

He forced his hands to leave the softness of her breasts. With uncharacteristic fumbling, he smoothed the waistband of her sweater back into place, then slowly, painfully, stepped away from her.

"No," he said.

She stared at him. "Tony?"

"No!"

"But—"

"This wasn't your fault," he said quietly, "it was mine. When I'm near you, Mercy, something happens, and I can't seem to stop myself from . . . But there's no excuse for my behavior. I explained to you before, in my kitchen, why you and I shouldn't . . . We're not—"

"We're not what, Tony?" Mercy interrupted, anger creeping into her voice. "Perfect? You're very big on that, aren't you, on everything being perfect? Well, 'perfect' is never going to happen when you're dealing with people, because you can't program them like pushing buttons on robots."

"I'm aware of that," he said, his voice rising to match hers. "Which is why, Miss Sloan, I don't enter into serious relationships where I have no choice but to stand around waiting to be stabbed in the back. I—Oh, hell. Forget it." He turned and strode to the windows, shoving his hands into his pockets and standing with his back to her.

Her head cocked, she stared at him, noting the rigid set of his shoulders. He'd erected his barrier again, she thought, shutting her out. But what he had just said revealed more than he probably realized.

Tony Murretti had been deeply hurt in the

past. How, when, where, and by whom, she had no idea, but that fact was becoming clearer with each new glimpse of his inner self.

And he was angry again, because once more he'd lost control with her. He preferred situations where his ever-famous "perfect" could be obtained, such as the building of his house, and now the addition of the landscaping. He must be a formidable opponent in the business arena, as he strove for, and no doubt achieved, perfection.

What sad secrets did his past contain? she wondered. What ghosts of pain haunted and tormented him, driving him in his quest for perfection? She wanted to run across the room and wrap her arms around him, promising him that she would never hurt him.

Why? she asked herself. Why was it so important that Tony believed in her, trusted her? Why did she constantly think about him when they were apart, and why did she so desperately want to make love with him when they were together?

She didn't know. The only thing of which she was certain was that she was not walking out of his life. There were too many questions, and she intended to find the answers. Somehow.

"Tony," she said, "you're assuming things about me that aren't quite true."

He turned to face her. "Oh?"

"Yes. I won't deny that I want a husband and

children. Where you're off the track is in thinking that I want that *now*."

"What do you mean?"

She didn't have the foggiest notion what she meant. She was winging this. She wanted answers, and she couldn't get them if he closed her out of his life.

"Sometime in the future," she said, "I'd like a family. But for Pete's sake, Tony, I'm only twenty-five. I have some living to do before I'm elbow-deep in diapers, dirty socks, and car pools. I fully intend to pursue my career, attain a reputation for expertise in my field, before I devote myself to a family. That way I'll be able to return to the work force once my children are in school."

This was great stuff, she thought smugly. She was really on a roll. Of course, Tony's frown was darkening with each sentence she spoke, which indicated he wasn't buying this malarkey, but it was the best she could do on such short notice.

She wasn't really lying to him, she reasoned. She simply wasn't telling him that she was already quite satisfied with her career accomplishments, and would be more than happy to fall in love and get married *now*. If she said that, however, Tony would immediately show her the door.

All was fair in love and war, Murretti, she told him silently. She wasn't certain yet if this was love, war, or absolutely nothing, but she most definitely intended to find out.

"Get the picture?" she asked, smiling brightly.

He crossed his arms over his chest and gazed intently at her. "Let me make sure we're on the same wavelength. The bottom line is that right now you'd be perfectly happy to have an affair with someone that lasts for"—he shrugged—"however long it lasts. Right?"

Not on your life, buster, Mercy thought.

"Absolutely right," she said.

Tony rubbed his chin. "That's very interesting. Of course, whoever you decide to bed-but-not-wed runs the risk of having their body broken by your brothers."

"Don't be silly. My brothers may be a teeny bit overprotective of me at times, but they don't run my life." She tossed her head. "I am an independent, professional, upwardly mobile woman of the nineties."

"Very, *very* interesting."

Something wasn't clicking into place, Tony mused. He had a prickly sensation at the back of his neck that said Mercy wasn't being completely honest. The words she was saying were music to his ears. What didn't wash was that it was Mercy Sloan saying them. He was going to stay on red alert and watch her carefully. In the meantime, there was no urgent need to hustle her out the door, and out of his life.

A sudden and natural smile broke across his

face. "I'll give this conversation serious thought, Mercy. As for now, I'm ready to sign a contract with Sloan Nursery and Landscaping. Then you can tell me more about my Christmas tree."

Four

Almost an hour later, Mercy decided that if business ever got slow at Sloan Nursery and Landscaping, she could moonlight as an actress. She was delivering her presentation to Tony with smooth expertise and a steady voice.

One of what she referred to as her "show-and-tell tools" was overlay transparencies, which allowed her to quickly and easily offer the client a variety of landscaping choices. She displayed the house edged by low bushes, then redwood tubs, then a flower bed constructed of narrow white block.

She answered Tony's multitude of questions with no hesitation, and was very impressed with his eye for detail. The lengthy discussion, she surmised, would appear to an observer as a strictly-business meeting.

What that observer would not be aware of was the physical and emotional turmoil within her that was in total contrast to her cool facade. She was speaking almost by rote, while carrying on a completely different inner dialogue.

What now? she asked herself. She'd set the stage with her declaration that her plans for getting married were far in the future. But what did Tony think about her grand speech? He'd seemed to relax, and was no longer determined to shove her out of his life. Did that mean the worldly and experienced Tony Murretti believed she was fully prepared to have a no-commitment, no-strings-attached affair with him?

Yes, that's what she'd said, all right, because he'd carefully double-checked by spelling it out loud and clear. And there she'd stood like an idiot bobbing her head up and down in agreement.

Oh, Lord, what now? she wondered yet again. She should hightail it out of there, put as much distance between herself and Tony as possible—and she knew without a shadow of a doubt that that was not what she was going to do.

"I think that covers it," she said at last. "You've made all the necessary selections, Tony. I'll work up a cost sheet for your review and get it to you by Monday afternoon. If it's acceptable, the information will be transferred to a contract ready for your signature."

"I don't intend to change my mind about what I've chosen, no matter what it costs," he said, getting to his feet. "It's perfect just the way it is. Attach the cost sheet to the contract, I'll sign it on Monday, and we can get this show on the road. Once I've made up my mind about something, I don't like delays." He turned to look down at her. "I know what I want, Mercy."

Mercy's whole body seemed to melt. *I know what I want, Mercy.* The words echoed in her mind as his dark soul-seeking gaze pinned her in place. *I know what I want, Mercy.* Oh, help!

She cleared her throat and began to push papers, pictures, and transparencies into her briefcase.

"Well, that's fine," she said, keeping her head down. "We at Sloan Nursery and Landscaping will be delighted to have you as a client." She snapped the briefcase closed and stood. Her gaze fixed on Tony's right shoulder, she smiled. "Thank you for your confidence in us, and be assured that every effort will be made to achieve the level of perfection that you're anticipating and expecting from us."

Tony glanced at his right shoulder, then chuckled. "My shoulder and I are duly impressed by that speech. If you keep talking to separate sections of my body, you'll eventually have carried on a conversation with every part of my anatomy." He raised his eyebrows. "Interesting thought."

Mercy glared at him, hoping her indignant expression would divert his attention from the fact that she was blushing like an adolescent.

He leaned toward her, grinning. "You're blushing."

"I certainly am not. It's just . . . just rather warm in here."

He nodded. "I see."

She shifted her briefcase to her left hand and extended her right, producing what she hoped was a pleasant smile.

He looked at her hand, then met her gaze.

"What's that?" he asked.

She frowned. "That's a hand, Mr. Murretti, with cute little fingers whose nails are polished with 'Chilled Watermelon.' You're supposed to shake said hand, indicating we've completed our business deal and that I'm leaving." She dropped her hand to her side. "Forget it. This is silly."

"It certainly is," he said, taking a step toward her. "We're far past the handshaking stage, Mercy Sloan. Life should move forward, not backward."

"Oh, well, I . . ."

"Don't you agree?"

"Yes, but . . ."

"Good."

He combed his fingers into her hair, holding

her head still, and captured her mouth with his. He parted her lips and his tongue met hers, instantly sending shock waves rocketing through her.

Shock waves were rolling through Tony too. Now that he knew he and Mercy wanted the same thing—an enjoyable but temporary affair—he could allow his passion full rein.

What he couldn't give her, she didn't even want at this point in her life. Later, with another man, she'd settle down and have babies. Babies that were created in the secret darkness of night, while making love . . . Dammit, some other man was going to make love to her, give her children!

He lifted his head and glared at Mercy. She opened her eyes and blinked, looking stunned at the abrupt ending of the sensuous kiss.

"Let's go get something to eat," he said gruffly.

She stepped back and matched his glowering expression.

"Is that an invitation or a command? Am I supposed to say, 'Yes, sir,' and salute?"

"Don't get sassy, Mercy." He strode behind his desk and snatched his suit coat from the back of the chair. "It's late, it's dinnertime, we both have to eat, so come on."

"No."

"What do you mean, 'No'?"

"It's clear enough. It's the opposite of 'yes.'

Why you're so irritated all of a sudden, I have no idea, but rude men are not my cup of tea as far as dinner companions go. Therefore, good night. I'll see you Monday with a contract and cost sheet ready for your signature." She moved around him and started toward the door.

Tony sighed and shook his head. "Mercy, wait a minute," he said quietly. "Please."

She stopped and looked at him over one shoulder. "Yes?"

"I'm sorry, okay? I did switch moods on you very quickly. Let me try again. Miss Sloan, would you do me the honor of sharing dinner with me?"

She smiled. "I'd be delighted, Mr. Murretti."

Tony's car was low, sleek, and silver, a sports coupe with an engine that rumbled like an animal eager to leap forward again each time he stopped at a red light.

Settled comfortably into the plush bucket seat, Mercy inhaled the delicious aroma of new leather. Tony commanded the powerful automobile with ease, allowing her to relax and enjoy the ride.

Well, that wasn't entirely true, she admitted. She couldn't *totally* relax when she was so acutely aware of the way Tony's hands, those same hands that had caressed her, gripped the steering wheel with nonchalant confidence.

And the way the muscles of his right leg bunched and stretched as he shifted from the brake to the gas pedal didn't lend itself to complete relaxation.

Then there was his aroma of after-shave and man, tantalizing her and overpowering the fragrance of the leather.

Truth be known, she thought glumly, she was a bundle of nerves, and probably on a collision course with emotional disaster.

"How about that steak house up ahead?" Tony asked, bringing Mercy from her thoughts. "It's not fancy, but the food is great."

"Perfect," she said.

He smiled. "One of my favorite words."

They were seated immediately, and had soon ordered steaks, baked potatoes, and vegetables, with a salad to start.

"This dressing is marvelous," Mercy said.

"It's their secret recipe," Tony said. "They sell it at the front counter."

"I should get a bottle for my parents. I know my dad would like it." She took another bite, then asked, "Do you have family, Tony? Parents? Brothers and sisters?"

"No."

"No one?"

"No." He looked at her for a long moment, then said, "Yes, I do have a mother. At least I assume she's still roaming around somewhere, but I haven't seen her in over thirty years." He shrugged. "So, for all practical purposes, I don't have any family."

"Your mother just disappeared?"

"Well, it's not all that dramatic, Mercy. She wasn't kidnapped or sold into white slavery. She put me in a state-funded home in the barrio area of Los Angeles when I was about five. She told me she'd be back in a few days, but that was the last I saw of her."

"Oh, Tony. I'm sorry."

He pushed his salad plate away and folded his arms on the top of the table.

"There's no need to be sorry," he said. "It was a lifetime ago. I've never told anyone before what she did. If someone presses the issue, I always just say I was orphaned young. Lord only knows why I spilled the truth to you." He shook his head. "But then I have a tendency to not act true to form when I'm with you."

"I'm honored that you shared it with me, Tony. Were you terribly unhappy in that home?"

"At first I was, I guess. I'd stand staring out the front window for hours at a stretch, waiting for her to come back. Somewhere along the line I faced the fact that she had no intention of doing that. There were about thirty kids in the home, all ages, and the neighborhood was rough. I grew up very quickly. It's not that big of a deal, Mercy. Let's just change the subject. I really don't care to discuss this."

The waitress arrived with their dinners before Mercy could reply. After she had left, Mercy made a major production of spreading butter and sour cream on her baked potato.

The potato would qualify for an artistic award, she thought, but she needed the time she lavished on it to digest what Tony had just revealed to her. She needed to reconcile the successful, self-confident man he was now with the sad, lonely, and betrayed little boy he had been.

She knew Tony would get angry if she broached the subject again. He was obviously none too happy with himself that he'd told her the story at all. This new glimpse of the real Tony Murretti revealed pain that touched the darkest and most desolate part of his soul. No wonder he kept a barrier around himself.

She kept her gaze fixed on her plate as she cut into her steak, not wishing to risk meeting his gaze. She simply wasn't certain what emotions might be readable in her eyes.

Tony slid a quick glance at Mercy as he sipped his water. She was engrossed in her dinner, thank heavens. It looked like she wasn't going to pursue the subject of his mother and his lousy childhood. He couldn't believe he'd told her about it in the first place. He'd been handling questions about his family for years, smoothly and coolly. Yet once again with Mercy, he acted completely out of character. He simply opened his big mouth and told her that his mother had dumped him in that home as though he were yesterday's garbage.

Why did she keep doing this to him? What strange power did she have over him that made him tell her things that nobody knew, made him kiss her when he'd promised himself he wouldn't, and made him feel things he damn well knew he shouldn't be feeling?

He didn't know, but he didn't like it, and it was going to stop. He just had to figure out how.

He considered and rejected several plans as he ate, finally settling on one when he'd nearly finished his steak.

Mercy had told him, in so many words, that she was willing to have an affair with him. Granted, his instincts were still warning him that something wasn't quite right, but he'd ignore that part. She'd declared her position, and that was that.

So, they would have an affair. He'd spend as much time with her as possible, and soon he would realize that she was just another woman. She might intrigue him now because she seemed so different from his former lovers, but he was sure her uniqueness would fade as he got to know her better. He'd get her out of his system and move on with his life.

It was a perfect plan.

"Are you enjoying your dinner, Mercy?" he asked when he was satisfied with his analysis.

"Yes, it's delicious. I'm glad you chose this place."

"So, tell me the schedule for my landscaping. I'll sign the contract Monday, then . . . ?"

"Well, first I bring in a crew to clear the area of weeds and debris. While that is being taken care of, I'll arrange to purchase what is needed to comply with your choices. I'll be on-site every day during the planting. When the job is completed, I'll give you instructions on the care of the lawn and all the plants and trees. Whether you tend to them yourself or hire a gardener is up to you. It will state in your contract that Sloan Nursery and Landscaping personnel will answer any questions you might have in the future. We don't forget our clients the minute the actual job is finished. We'll always be available for you."

"That's comforting," he said, smiling. "I just pick up the phone and you'll come running. For whatever I need."

Oh, blast, Mercy thought, she was blushing again. She had to stop doing that if she was going to follow through on her let's-have-an-affair-for-however-long-it-lasts plan.

Was she really capable of doing that? she wondered. Probably not, but she had no intention of exiting stage left from Tony's life yet. All she could do was take this a moment at a time, do whatever felt right, and hope she didn't end up crying for five years straight when it was over.

"That's correct, Mr. Murretti," she said, deciding to bat her eyelashes as an afterthought. "I'm available for"—she looked directly into his eyes—"for whatever you need."

Heat rocketed through Tony's body. Sensual images flitted across his mental vision of Mercy naked in his bed, lifting her arms to welcome him into her embrace. She was his for the taking, and it would be ecstasy.

"Dessert tonight?" their waitress asked, suddenly appearing beside the table.

"No," Tony said. He wanted to leave, get Mercy alone, and—

"Yes," Mercy said. She needed a little more time to gather her courage for whatever this night would bring.

The waitress handed her a menu, and she read the extensive dessert selection.

Oh, dear, she thought. She had eaten every bite of her dinner, and didn't have room for the smallest, simplest dessert, let alone the lavish creations described. Well, she'd just have to fake it.

"I'll have Black Forest cake and coffee, please," she said, handing the menu back to the waitress.

"Coming right up," the woman said.

"No rush," Mercy said quickly. "Take your

time. Just meander back over this way when the mood strikes."

The waitress gave her a perplexed look, then walked away. A busboy materialized and removed their plates. Mercy inwardly groaned as the waitress returned almost immediately with a huge slice of chocolate cake covered in whipped cream and cherries, the red cherry sauce running in thick rivers over the cake.

Mercy stared at the dessert in horror for a long moment, then plastered a smile on her face and met Tony's gaze again.

"Doesn't that look scrumptious?" she said brightly. "Feel free to share it with me. You still have a fork there. Help yourself."

"No, thank you. I really couldn't eat another thing. You certainly have a healthy appetite for such a small person."

"Don't I, though?" she said weakly, her smile fading. "I can eat more than the brothers Sloan sometimes." She picked up her fork. "Well, here I go, plowing right into this grotesque . . . I mean, gorgeous confection. I wonder who named this Black Forest? It doesn't make any sense at all because—"

"Mercy."

"Yes?"

"Eat the cake."

"Right."

Tony propped one elbow on the table and rested his chin on his fist. He adopted an expression of total concentration, as if he were about to witness a major-breakthrough experiment.

As Mercy scooped up a forkful of cake, whipped cream, and cherries, Tony watched the fork rise, turn, then the prongs disappear into Mercy's mouth. The end of the fork reappeared, sans the food, and was lowered to the plate.

Then Mercy chewed, and chewed, and chewed.

Tony raised his eyebrows questioningly. "Good?" he asked.

"Mmm," she said, nodding and chewing.

"That's nice." He paused. "At the rate you're going, I figure you'll polish off the whole piece in about three weeks or so."

She glared at him . . . and chewed.

Swallow, Mercy told herself. But she didn't want this sweet, sticky mess. She was clinging to the asinine hope that if she chewed long enough, her stomach would get the message that something had to move over and make room for this glop. If Tony weren't sitting there staring at her, she might be able to find a potted plant to dump the cake into.

She swallowed at last, took a quick sip of coffee, then held the fork a hovering half inch above the cake. Sighing, she plunked the fork onto the table.

"I quit," she said, moaning. "If I have one more bite, the end result will be the same as when Drew took me on a ferris wheel when I was eight years old, and I'd just had two hot dogs, three cotton candies, and a Jolly Orange Jubilee drink. Believe me, it was *not* a pretty picture."

Tony chuckled and signaled to the waitress for the check.

"Do you want a doggie bag," he asked, "so that you can bring your dessert along for later?"

"No!"

"I didn't think so."

"I shouldn't have ordered it," she admitted. "I'm sorry that I wasted it."

Tony's smile faded. "Why *did* you order it, Mercy?"

"Oh, well, I thought I wanted it. You know, a yummy dessert after a delicious dinner. It certainly is a work of art, and on another occasion I . . . would eat . . . every bite . . . Why are you looking at me so strangely?"

"Am I? Well, I guess I was wondering if you might have ordered that cake to delay leaving here . . . with me. Just the two of us . . . together."

"Don't be absurd." She averted her eyes from his and made a precise square out of her napkin. "Of course we're leaving here together, just the two of us. After all, that's how we arrived, so how else would we leave? I certainly don't have a problem with that, Tony." She looked at him again.

"Well, it was just a thought. Since I was off base, I won't hesitate to ask if you'd like to—"

"Your check, sir," the waitress said. "You can pay up front at the cashier's counter. Have a nice night."

"Thank you," Tony said. "It was a delicious meal." He stood and dropped several bills on the table for the tip. "Ready, Mercy?"

She nodded, and proceeded him to the exit. She was scarcely aware of where she was going, though, for she was trying to figure out what he'd been about to say.

I won't hesitate to ask if you'd like to . . . Like to what? Tear off her clothes and make whoopee in the backseat of his car? That was dumb. His car didn't *have* a backseat. What then? Go to his house or to her apartment and. . . ? Rob a bank? Mug a mugger?

Mercy Sloan, she admonished herself, calm down. Tony would tell her soon enough what he had in mind for the remainder of the evening. Good Lord, in a couple of minutes he was going to announce what he had in mind for the remainder of the evening! *Mercy, knock it off.*

Tony paid the bill, then placed one hand lightly at the small of Mercy's back and escorted her out of the restaurant. He noticed that she was moving stiffly, as if she wasn't sure she should be doing this. She could deny it from there to Sunday, he thought as he assisted her into his car, but he'd still believe that her ordering the dessert had been a delaying tactic. She was a nervous wreck, obviously worried about what was, or was not, on the agenda for the rest of the night.

He should take her back to his office to get her car, he told himself as he walked around to the driver's side. Then he'd follow her home, wave a farewell, and disappear.

No, dammit, he mentally argued, she was a grown woman, capable of making a decision about who she would or would not sleep with. It wasn't *his* responsibility to figure out if she truly knew what she was getting herself into. *He* wasn't one of her bodyguard brothers.

Not even close, he thought, as he slid behind the wheel and turned the key in the ignition. The strong urge of passion that stirred within him whenever he was near her was far from a brotherly feeling. No, he was a man who desired the woman sitting next to him.

Gripping the steering wheel with more force than was necessary, he skillfully maneuvered the sleek car into the traffic. When he had to stop at a red light, he drummed his fingers impatiently on the leather-wrapped wheel.

One more mile, he thought, and he'd have to decide what he was going to do. Take her back to his office building to collect her car, or . . .

Dammit, he inwardly fumed. What was his problem? He was acting like a gawky adolescent

who didn't know if he should kiss the cheer-
leader good night at her door.

It was that damnable sense of protection he
felt toward Mercy, along with all those other
unwelcome emotions she roused in him, that
were causing his irrational behavior. He was fed
up with his indecision. Enough was enough.

The light turned green, and he pressed his
foot heavily on the gas.

"How about a nightcap on my boat?" he
asked, his grip on the steering wheel tightening
until his knuckles were white.

This was it, Mercy thought, her heart beating
wildly. This was the "what" that completed the
sentence, "I won't hesitate to ask you if you'd
like to . . ." It was decision time.

He owned a boat? she mused, delaying that
decision. She could remember sitting in the
restaurant with Clark, waiting for the then
unknown Tony Murretti and admiring the boats
in the marina. She'd even said how lovely it
would be to escape from the stress of the city on
one of the cabin cruisers.

And Tony owned a boat. A floating, all-by-
itself, no-neighbors-around boat. It did not, at
the moment, conjure up an image of blissful
escape. Panic was closer to the mark.

"Mercy?"

"Huh? Oh. A boat. A nightcap on a boat
sounds . . . interesting. Certainly. Why not?

That's exactly what we'll do. We'll go have a nightcap on your boat."

"Fine."

She slid a glance at Tony from beneath her lashes. She could actually feel the tension emanating from him. It was tangible, crackling through the air. That didn't make sense. Why would a slick guy like Tony, a worldly, been-around-the-block man, be uptight about taking a woman to his boat?

Men were mysteries, she deduced, enigmas that sent out conflicting, confusing signals. Then again, women weren't all that easy to figure out, either. For some reason, the fact that Tony was tense allowed her to feel calm and in control of herself. Figure that one.

As Tony sped toward the marina where he kept his boat, his frown deepened and a stress-induced headache pounded painfully in his temples.

At the same time, Mercy burrowed comfortably into her plush seat, watching the city lights whiz by and making no attempt to erase her complacent smile.

If Mercy had any doubts about Tony's success as a financial investor, the marina erased them. It was an obviously exclusive place with a twenty-four-hour guard who manned the tall, metal grillwork gate that sat across the marina's entrance.

Tony produced what appeared to be a credit card from his wallet and handed it to the uniformed man. The card was inserted into some device that Mercy could not clearly see, then the heavy gate swung open.

"Enjoy the evening," the guard said, giving the card back to Tony. "It's certainly a nice night to be on the water, Mr. Murretti."

"Yes, it is," Tony said. "Thank you."

He drove through the gate, and a minute later parked in a paved lot. After assisting Mercy from the car, he nodded toward the multitude of boats in the distance. Without speaking they began walking toward the boats, careful not to let their bodies touch.

Amber lights on tall poles cast a soft glow over the walkway that fronted the slips where boats of every size and design imaginable bobbed gently in the dark water.

Mercy inhaled deeply, mentally sorting through the intriguing scents that assaulted her—the tangy salt water, a slight odor of fish, and the aroma of fresh lemons, which she surmised came from decks polished to a mirror finish.

"Heavenly," she said.

"Pardon me?"

"The aromas. They're a wonderful mixture. It's also beautiful here, so serene and peaceful.

And the boats are magnificent, lined up like horses at the gate."

Tony glanced around. "I never paid much attention to any of that. That must be the artist in you. You see things that other people just take for granted."

"Maybe, but I think it would be difficult for anyone to take this setting for granted. Well, I suppose you would if you're used to elegance like this."

"Believe me, Mercy," he said, a slight edge to his voice, "I've earned every bit of what I possess. None of it was handed to me on a silver platter. I still work very hard to protect what's now mine. What I have I intend to keep."

"You acquired it alone," she said quietly, "and you guard it alone."

"Yes."

"Don't you ever get lonely?"

"No."

"But . . ."

"Here's my boat."

They stopped, and Mercy's gaze swept over the cabin cruiser. It was larger than she'd expected, perhaps forty-five feet long, with front and rear decks, and a covered controls area. The brass railings sparkled in the lamplight, and portholes dotted the lower level.

"Oh, Tony," she said, "it's magnificent. Absolutely beautiful."

"She. It's a 'she,' not an 'it.'" His voice gentled.

"Yes, she's quite a lady, isn't she? The minute I saw her I knew I had to have her."

"I can understand why. What's her name?"

"It's painted on the stern, per regulations, but it's there by the cabin, too, on that life ring."

She leaned forward to read the name, then frowned. It was somewhat disturbing to see the word in bold print.

Tony's cabin cruiser was called *Perfection*.

Five

Mercy didn't know diddly about boats. But she did recognize luxurious when she saw it, and the *Perfection* definitely qualified as luxurious.

The walls of the area below deck were paneled in dark wood, and the furniture, which was bolted to the floor, was mahogany. The prevailing color was royal blue, with accents of a paler blue and white.

The center of the area was a multipurpose room where meals were served and people could gather for conversation. The padded benches lining the walls, Tony explained to her, could be converted into beds for extra guests.

The master stateroom was behind a door in the stern of the boat. The galley was set in the center, beyond the central area, and in the bow of the boat was a smaller stateroom with its own head. The entire floor was covered in blue carpeting.

"It's exquisite," Mercy said, then threw up her hands. "I've run out of words of praise. She has justified her name, and then some. Did you decorate it, or was it like this when you bought it?"

"Three years ago when I first saw her, the color scheme was pink. Bright pink. I liked everything else as far as size, lines, the layout, so I had it redecorated. She deserved to be perfect."

Mercy nodded, then looked down as she ran her fingertips across the top of a butter-soft leather chair. Slowly she lifted her gaze to meet his.

"Tony, why is perfection so important to you? I'm not criticizing, I'm just wondering. It's also none of my business, so feel free to ignore the question. You did say that you realize you can't program people to be perfect, but I imagine you expect them to be very close to it, and have little patience with those who aren't."

She swept one arm in the air. "This boat, your home, the landscaping we'll do for you, the decor of your office . . . are all nonhuman entities that are, in your mind, perfect. Why? Why are you so intensely adamant about perfection?"

A flash of anger crossed Tony's face, and his

jaw tightened as he narrowed his eyes. Mercy continued to directly meet his gaze. Several long and silent seconds passed before he spoke.

"As you once said, Mercy, perfection is subjective. I can't explain something to you that is relative only to *my* personal measuring stick."

"In other words," she said, "it's none of my business."

He started to retort, then shook his head. Shrugging out of his suit coat, he tossed it onto a chair, then dragged a restless hand through his hair.

"It figures," he said dryly. "None of the people who work for me, none of my acquaintances, none of the women I've dated have ever questioned my demand for perfection. They're aware of it, I'm sure, but they simply accept it as a part of who I am. But you? You want to know why." A smile tugged at the corners of his lips. "Yes, it figures."

"Well, I . . ." Mercy started, but her voice trailed off. She cocked her head to one side. "You make me sound like a nosy old busybody."

His smile broadened into a grin, and a chuckle rumbled in his chest.

"Now you wait just a darn minute here," she said, her eyes flashing. She marched around a table to stand in front of him, tilting her head back so she could glower at him. "I am *not* nosy, Mr. Murretti. Did it ever occur to you that I'm trying to understand you, know who you are, because I care about you? No, of course not. You immediately decide I'm simply nosy about everything and everyone. Well, you're wrong."

He blinked in surprise at her tirade, and his smile disappeared.

"Furthermore," she rushed on, "you keep harping on the fact that you don't act true to form around me, and you're not thrilled about it. You're ticked off as though *your* behavior is *my* fault. Well, fine, but tit for tat. I have never before in my life been thrown so off balance by a man as I am by you, and it's getting very irritating. I am not, Murretti, accustomed to daydreaming about what it would be like to make love with . . . a man . . . who . . ."

Her eyes widened and her hands flew to her suddenly flushed cheeks.

"Oh, good Lord," she said. "I have the biggest mouth in Santa Barbara, in the entire state of California, in the whole United States of America. Inform my family that I adore them and I'll miss them, because I'm about to die of embarrassment." She dropped her hands and sighed. "Tell Drew he can have my collection of baseball cards."

Tony grasped her shoulders, and his voice was gentle and low when he spoke.

"You are something, Mercy Sloan. I've never met anyone like you before. I really don't know what to do about you, so, for now, I'm going to kiss you."

"Oh" was all Mercy managed to say.

It was a feather-light kiss, a mere brushing of the lips, yet it sent a shiver coursing through Mercy as her mind, heart, and body demanded more, much more.

Tony wrapped his arms around her and pulled her tight against him. He captured her mouth, and she surrendered totally, kissing him back with all the soaring passion in her.

She was going to make love with Tony Murretti, she thought hazily. Their union would be beautiful. Their becoming one would be . . . perfect.

She ended the kiss and whispered, "I'm not daydreaming, Tony. This is real, and now, and I want to make love with you more than I can begin to tell you."

"I want you too," he said, his voice hoarse. "But I have to know that you're thinking clearly, that you're absolutely certain that . . . Dammit, here I go again, doing what I don't do. I do *not* make speeches to women regarding whether or not they're certain they want to make love. Women are intelligent and fully capable of making decisions, of having control of their bodies, their entire lives, their . . . It's not *my* responsibility to put them through the third degree before . . . Good Lord, I'm babbling. I don't babble. I've never babbled in my life."

Mercy laughed softly, then gave him a quick kiss on the lips.

"I must say," she said, still smiling, "for a novice babbler you're doing a superb job of it."

For some unknown reason, Mercy realized in wonder, Tony was hesitating about their making love. The man was actually losing it right before her eyes. And as had happened in the car, the more tense *he* became, the calmer and more determined *she* became.

Any lingering doubts she'd had about taking this important intimate step with Tony were gone, along with the nervous flutter in the pit of her stomach. To make love with Tony Murretti was right, and good, and was definitely meant to be.

"Tony," she whispered, then flicked the tip of her tongue across his lower lip. A groan rumbled in his chest. "I want you, Tony. You babbled very nicely, but let's get back to what we were doing." Her busy little tongue repeated its provocative journey over his lip. "Yes?"

"Yes." He stiffened. "No. No, wait." He grabbed her shoulders and inched her away from his aching, aroused body. "Stay."

A bubble of laughter escaped from her.

"Stay?" she repeated. "What's next? Heel? Roll over? Fetch the newspaper? I feel like a cocker spaniel." Her smile faded. "Tony, this is about as romantic as yesterday's oatmeal. Are you . . . are you trying to break it to me gently that you don't want me, don't want to make love with me?"

"No!" he nearly yelled. "I want you so damn much, I'm about to explode."

"Then what's the problem here?"

"It's the damn PTA!" he hollered, flinging out his arms.

"Oh, good Lord," she said, covering her heart with one hand. "You scared the bejeebers out of me." She drew a steadying breath, then squinted at him. "It's the damn what?"

He lowered his chin to his chest and closed his eyes.

"Tony?" Mercy said tentatively.

He shook his head, then looked at her, his hands planted on his hips. He definitely was *not* smiling.

"My mind, Miss Sloan," he said, his words slow and measured, "is mush." Her eyes widened as she stared at him. "You have driven me to within an inch of insanity."

"Me?" She folded her arms over her breasts and glared at him, adding an indignant little sniff. "I did no such thing. If you're going to accuse me of an atrocity, you best be prepared to produce firm evidence. Just exactly what did I do?"

"You were born!"

"Would you quit yelling? You're rocking the boat." She paused. "Was that a pun? Oh, well."

She frowned at him again. "You're not making one bit of sense."

"See? I told you. I've probably already gone over the edge." He took a deep breath. "Okay, I'm fine now. I'm totally in charge."

"How nice for you."

"Mercy, look, let me try to explain. Not that it's all that clear to me. I can only tell you what I surmise happened."

"May I sit down?"

"Oh, of course. Would you like something to eat, or drink?"

She sat in one of the leather chairs by a round mahogany table. "No, thank you. I'm still trying to erase the memory of Black Forest cake from my brain."

Tony sat down beside her, facing her profile. He leaned over, bringing his face close to hers as she turned her head to look at him.

Their eyes met, and once more desire raged like a wildfire within them, as though a match had been set to dry timber.

Such heat, Mercy thought, unable to tear her gaze from Tony's. She was aflame. Her breasts ached for his touch, and the rapid beating of her heart was matched by the throbbing need deep and low within her.

She would not have one moment of regret, she knew, after making love with Tony. Eventually her false stand on no-commitment affairs would probably be exposed, and Tony would sweep out of her life like a bat out of hell. She was setting herself up for guaranteed heartbreak, but she didn't care. Not now, not on this night.

This night. She and Tony had come so close, *so close,* to making love, to sharing the ultimate intimacy. It would have been the glorious number three of her four wondrous events with Tony. Meeting him had been number one, and their first kisses were two.

But he'd called a halt to the lovemaking, and his reasons were totally confusing. He'd brought this night back to reality with a thud. This night was not turning out to be terrific.

"The floor," she said, barely managing to keep her voice steady, "is yours."

He tore his gaze from hers and stared at the ceiling for a moment. "Mercy, I told you that I learned early in my life how to quickly analyze people. It was imperative, because in the neighborhood where I grew up you might not get a second chance if you gauged someone wrong the first time. I rarely, if ever, make a mistake when I meet someone."

"That first day we met, I came to conclusions about you, about who you are and what you want from life, and I immediately knew that we were total opposites."

"But . . ."

He straightened and raised one hand. "Let me

finish, okay? I have to sort through this a bit as I go along."

"All right," she said softly. "I'm sorry I interrupted."

"You really threw me this evening when you said my conclusions about you were right, but the timing was wrong. You do want a normal family life, but not now. Later."

Oh, good grief, Mercy thought. Tony's strange behavior was all because of her teeny-tiny fib? Who was she kidding? It was definitely a big lie, and she was already beginning to pay the piper.

"Mercy," Tony went on, "I honestly can't remember when I've been so off the mark. I've always thought my ability to judge people was nearly perfect."

There was that word again! Mercy thought crossly. Tony and his damnable 'perfect.' Any niggling pokes from her conscience that she should confess her lie flew out the window . . . or porthole, rather. It would do Tony good to eat some humble pie, to face the fact that in certain circumstances, he was not perfect.

"You can't win them all," she said pleasantly. "Even a pro like you is bound to have an off day. You might as well accept your defeat graciously. You were right about me to a certain extent, but with something like this, the wrong timing can create a completely different scenario. The bottom line is, you really blew it."

Oh, she was rotten, Mercy thought. Talk

about pouring salt on his male-ego wound. But what did all this have to do with his calling a halt to their lovemaking? Darned if *she* knew. Well, when you want to know something . . .

"I'm confused," she said. "What does when I intend to go to PTA meetings have to do with you suddenly stopping our . . . the"—she waved one arm through the air—"what we were doing?"

"I'm unraveling that," he said. "I think perhaps a part of my mind is still set on my first impression of you. I can't get past it, even though I've been told I was wrong. So, there I was, about to make love with a woman who wants marriage. Therefore, I couldn't do it."

"Oh."

"That's it? Just 'Oh'?"

"Well, for heaven's sake, Tony, what do you expect me to say? This whole subject is being discussed so clinically, it's as romantic as a dead fish. Your need for perfection is tripping you up. You seem unable to deal with the fact that you made a mistake."

"It was a new and disturbing experience," he said, a slight edge to his voice.

"And so, now what? We took time out, got you all squared away, and now we'll pick up where we left off? No, thank you. I'd like to go home, please."

"You're angry," he said, sounding surprised.

She sighed. "I don't know what I am. This

whole scene is bizarre. I think it would be best if we just put paid to this evening."

"If that's what you want, then that's what we'll do." He got to his feet and extended his hand to her. She placed hers in his, and allowed him to draw her up close to him. "But I would like to see you again. Tomorrow night?"

No, no, no, Mercy thought. Everything was going haywire. No wonder her parents had harped on the lesson of, 'Never tell lies,' while she'd been growing up. She should gather the few precious memories of her time with Tony, and decline any further social invitations from him.

"How about it, Mercy? Tomorrow night?" Tony asked again. He wrapped his arms around her. "There's a big-band concert in one of the parks. I can bring a picnic supper, you can bring your lovely self, and we'll go. Eight o'clock. Say yes."

Say no, Mercy told herself.

"Yes," she said.

Tony brushed his lips over hers. "Good. I'll take you to your car now, then I'm going to follow you home."

"You don't have to do that. I live in the opposite direction from your house. I'll be perfectly safe driving to my apartment."

"I'll follow you home, Mercy."

"Well, you've obviously gone into a stubborn mode, so I won't argue the point."

"Smart lady."

"A lady who grew up with three older brothers. I recognize a male I'm-not-going-to-budge-on-this statement when I hear it."

Tony chuckled, then sobered. "Mercy, I hope you know that I wanted you tonight, wanted to make love with you very much. I still do. Lord knows, I still do."

"I wanted you, too, Tony," she said softly. But it was so dangerous, she thought. What if she fell in love with this man? What if she began to imagine him as her husband, the father of her children? She should end this right now—but she couldn't. If she was left with a broken heart, she'd have no one to blame but herself. "And I still want you."

He kissed her on the forehead. "Perfect. Come on, I'll drive you to your car."

Outside on the walkway, Mercy stopped for a moment to look at Tony's boat. Her gaze came to rest on the life ring that boasted the cruiser's name.

Perfection, she mused. If Tony Murretti knew just how far from perfection their relationship was, he'd toss her into the brink.

"Ready?" he asked.

"What? Oh, yes, of course."

He circled her shoulders with one arm, and they walked slowly back to the car, both lost in their own thoughts.

· · ·

Hours later, Tony flipped back the sheet and left the bed, muttering several earthy expletives. Naked, he strode across his bedroom to one of the windows on the far wall. He yanked open the drapes and braced his hands high on the window frame, gazing out at the star-studded sky.

He couldn't sleep . . . again. To be more precise, he couldn't sleep again because of Mercy Sloan. What a fiasco he'd made of their time together on the *Perfection*. He still found it incredibly hard to believe that he'd been the one to call a halt to what he knew would have been exquisitely beautiful lovemaking with Mercy.

But he had stopped it, and had an ache in his gut and blood still pounding in his veins as evidence of that fact.

"Dammit," he said, smacking the window frame with the heel of one hand.

What in the hell was the matter with him? he asked himself for the umpteenth time. The explanation he'd given Mercy made sense, he supposed. He definitely was not accustomed to making mistakes. In fact, he made few mistakes in any area of his life, for he'd learned early on that there was little room for error if a man wanted to emerge on the top of the heap.

For all that, what he'd said to Mercy, his excuse for ending their lovemaking, had been a bunch of bull.

Sure, he'd like to believe it, because then he might actually get some sleep. And he could get Miss Mercy Sloan into his bed the following night after the outdoor concert.

But his instincts, which had held him in good stead for many years, were announcing loud and clear that things were not as they seemed. Something just wasn't right about Mercy.

Until he had all the pieces to the puzzle sorted and put firmly in their proper place, until he knew that all was perfect, as it should be, he would not make love with Mercy.

"Hell," he said, and stalked back to his bed.

The first dim glow of dawn was inching over the horizon before Tony finally slept.

Fingers of early morning sunlight tiptoed across Mercy's face insisting that she awaken. She groaned and drew the sheet up over her head, willing herself to drift back into blissful slumber. Within minutes she knew she was defeated, and yanked the sheet down, her hands thudding heavily onto the mattress.

She was in a heap of trouble, she thought. She had told Tony a bold-faced lie, and it was already circling around to demand its due. Well, what was done was done. If she confessed now that she positively was *not* interested in having a fling with Tony, he would very politely and very firmly show her the door. If she didn't confess, she'd end up making love with him, and probably lose her heart to him.

"What a mess," she said aloud.

She pursed her lips and frowned up at the ceiling.

So, what was she going to do? she asked herself. Confess, or keep silent? Go, or stay? Grab hold of a handful of happiness while it was within her reach, or take the safer road and retreat from Tony?

This was dumb, she decided. The emotions churning within her were far stronger than any sense of reality or measure of sound reasoning. Why torment herself with questions when she already knew the answers?

She was *not* going to walk out of Tony Murretti's life. Not yet. She was *not* going to confess her falsehood and get herself tossed out, either. She *was* going to make love with him, and let the chips of her broken heart simply fall where they may.

Nodding decisively, she threw back the sheet and swung her feet to the floor. A soft smile touched her lips as images of Tony flitted across her mental vision like an enticing movie.

Tonight, tonight, tonight, her heart sang, she would become one with Tony, and she knew it would be beautiful beyond description.

Nothing stood in the way of their lovemaking, and the realization of what would take place felt right, and good, and deliciously warm.

"Tonight, Tony," she whispered, "is ours."

Six

After many muttered and mumbled opinions, and the rejection of six outfits, Mercy settled on what to wear to the outdoor concert—dark blue slacks and a pale blue short-sleeve top. The top had a round neckline and covered snaps down the entire front.

She closed the row of snaps all the way up, then undid the top two and studied her reflection in the bathroom mirror.

"Go for it," she said, then freed two more snaps. "Tsk, tsk, you wanton woman you."

Her hair was newly trimmed to assure no chance of it going boing, and she'd brushed it until it shone. Her makeup was light, as usual, and she'd generously sprayed her floral cologne across her neck and wrists.

White sandals were buckled into place, revealing toenails polished with 'Chilled Watermelon.' Necessary this and that went into a casual blue canvas shoulder bag, and she was ready to go to the park with Tony.

She was ready for a lot more than that with Tony, she thought merrily.

She left her bedroom and wandered around the living room, fluffing a pillow that was already fluffed, straightening magazines that were neat as a pin, checking the soil in her multitude of plants that she'd watered that morning.

She fiddled and fussed until she finally sighed and sank onto the pale yellow sofa.

Darn it, she thought, she was nervous. How dare she be nervous? She knew exactly what she was doing, was comfortable with her decision, and was anticipating the evening ahead with an eagerness that was almost shameful. Therefore, the squad of butterflies in her stomach could just zoom off to Toledo and leave her alone.

She absolutely, positively *refused* to be nervous.

A knock sounded at the door.

"Ohmigod!" She snatched up a throw pillow and hugged it to her breasts. "I'm not home. I'm really not."

The knock was repeated.

"Stop it, Mercy Sloan," she said. She smacked

the pillow back into place, got to her feet, and marched across the room. Hesitating for a moment, she drew a steadying breath, produced a hopefully calm smile, and opened the door. "Well, hello and good evening . . ." She blinked. "Clark?"

"Hi, baby sister," Clark said, walking past her into the room.

Mercy closed the door and turned to frown at her brother. "Clark, what are you doing here?"

"Did you break a bottle of perfume or something?" he asked. "It smells like a flower shop in here."

"Forget that. Why are you in my living room?"

"It was my turn to work at the nursery this evening, and a late call came in for you. Since I was going right by your place, I decided to deliver the message personally. Your crew for Murretti's is all set for Monday morning."

"Fine. Thank you. Good-bye."

"My date for tonight has the flu," Clark went on, oblivious to her glare, "so I thought I'd see if you wanted to go out for pizza. Do you want to? I'm buying, big spender that I am."

"I can't, Clark, but I appreciate the invitation. I'm leaving in a few minutes."

"You have a date?"

"Well, yes, so if you'd kindly just shuffle off to Buffalo . . ."

"Who are you going out with?"

"Clark, I'm twenty-five, not fifteen."

He held up his hands in a gesture of peace. "Hey, I'm not checking up on you. I'm interested because I care about you. Who's the lucky guy? Greg What's-his-name?"

"No, not Greg What's-his-name. He's a walking, talking computer. If the conversation isn't centered on RAM, or ROM, or floppy disks, or whatever, he's lost and has nothing at all to say."

"Oh, that's too bad. Well, cross him off your list. So? Who's on for tonight?"

"Clark, go eat pizza. The anchovies are calling to you. Go, go." She flapped her hands at him.

Clark frowned and folded his arms over his chest. "You're trying to hustle me out of here. Why? What's the big secret about your date?"

"There's no secret," she said. "I just don't like the impression your being here gives. I mean, for Pete's sake, it looks like you're going to pass judgment on my date. I hate to be rude, Clark, but haul your tush out of my apartment."

"Okay, okay," he said, starting toward the door. Mercy was right behind him. "You don't have to get hostile. I know when I'm not loved, wanted, or appreciated. I'll just slink off like a neglected dog and—"

"Out, Sloan."

He shot her a glare over his shoulder, then opened the door. He stopped so quickly that Mercy bumped into him. She peered around him to see why he'd halted his exit.

Tony Murretti stood beyond the open doorway, one hand lifted, prepared to knock on the door.

"Tony?" Clark said.

"Oh, darn and damn," Mercy said under her breath.

"Hello, Clark," Tony said, dropping his hand to his side. He tilted his head to see Mercy, still nearly totally concealed behind her brother. "Good evening, Mercy."

"Hi," she said, smiling weakly. Despite her brother's presence, she allowed herself a few seconds of gawking. Tony Murretti in jeans and a white knit shirt was a sight to behold. A body that had been appealing in tailored business suits was downright mouth watering in casual clothes. Those shoulders, that chest, those arms, those legs . . . Glorious. "I . . . um . . . Come in, Tony."

"I would," he said, "but you two are blocking the doorway."

"Clark, move," Mercy said, tugging on her brother's shirt.

"What?" Clark said. "Oh, yeah." He stepped back. Tony entered the apartment and Clark shut the door. "Is this a business call, Tony? Mercy has a date, but I might be able to answer your questions. You and I could go get a pizza too."

"Clark," Mercy said, before Tony could answer, "Tony is aware that I'm going out because he's the one I'm going out with."

"No," Clark said, folding his arms across his chest again, "you're not."

Tony chuckled. "Well now, this ought to be interesting."

Mercy gave her brother a hard, meaningful stare. "Clark, go stuff your face with pizza."

"We'd better be on our way now, Mercy," Tony said pleasantly. "We wouldn't want to miss any of the concert, you know."

"Concert?" Clark said. "What kind of concert? One with a heavy metal band, where people stand on their chairs and scream, then trample victims under their feet? Are you nuts, Murretti?"

"It's an outdoor concert, Clark," Mercy said. "Not that it's any of your business."

"Oh," Clark said. "So you'll go to a park and sit on a blanket on the ground in the dark . . . and no one will pay any attention to what's happening on the blanket next to theirs. One of *those* concerts?"

"Yep," Tony said.

"No," Clark said.

Mercy groaned with frustration. "I don't believe this. Clark Sloan, you're making a fool of yourself *and* me. You're acting as though you just beamed in from the eighteen hundreds. Would you please leave?"

"No, I won't," Clark said, none too quietly. "I

warned you about him, Mercy. I said he was a really nice guy, but much too experienced for you. He's been around far too many blocks." He looked quickly at Tony. "No offense, Tony, but you get the drift, right?" He redirected his attention to a glowering Mercy. "There was a time when you listened to your big brothers, Mercy. You apparently don't think you need to do that anymore, but it's quite obvious that you most certainly do."

Tony raised his eyebrows and looked at Mercy. "Miss Sloan, do you care to address that last remark by Mr. Sloan?" Amusement danced in his dark eyes, and he was obviously struggling not to laugh.

"Stay out of this, Tony," Mercy said crossly. "This is humiliating. Clark, I'm going to murder you. It's as simple as that. You've also just insulted a very important client of Sloan Nursery and Landscaping, who has not—read my lips, idiot—has *not* yet signed a contract."

"I don't care," Clark yelled. "You're more important than money. This guy is out of your league, and it's part of my job description as a big brother to protect you from men like him."

"Okay, that's enough," Tony said, raising one hand. All traces of humor had left his face. "I respect what you're doing, Clark, even if it is old-fashioned. I also admire anyone who can size up a person the way you pegged me. I've admittedly been down a street or two."

"My point exactly," Clark said.

"However," Tony went on, "that doesn't automatically mean I don't know when to shift gears. Mercy is absolutely safe with me."

"I am not," Mercy said, planting her fists on her hips. "I really resent that, Tony Murretti. I am *not* absolutely safe with you."

"You're not?" Tony and Clark said in unison.

"No, I am not! To say that I am, Mr. Murretti, is rude, insulting, demeaning, and a derogatory statement regarding my femininity and womanly appeal."

"Huh?" Tony and Clark said, once again in chorus.

"What are you insinuating, Tony?" Mercy asked. "That when you're alone with me you feel like a protective big brother? Oh, ha! I was on your boat last night, remember? I was the one you—"

"Oh, Lord," Tony interrupted. He clamped a hand over Mercy's mouth. Fury radiated from her eyes like laser beams. "Would you please slow down and think?"

"What boat?" Clark asked. "What last night? What happened?"

"Nothing happened," Tony said. "Right, Mercy?" She glared at him. "Nod your head." She didn't. "Mercy, if Clark takes a swing at me, I'm going to defend myself. His then broken nose will be on your conscience."

"Hey, now wait just a damn minute," Clark

said. "You're not dealing with some lightweight here. I can take care of myself."

Tony turned his head and pinned Clark in place with a cold, steady stare.

"Yeah, well," Clark mumbled, "I'm a bit rusty when it comes to punch and run. In my day, though, no one messed with me." He ran a finger down his nose. "Broken, huh?"

"In spades," Tony said.

"Well, a man's gotta do, what he's gotta do. Take your hand off Mercy's mouth, Murretti, so she can tell me why she's not safe with you because of what happened on your boat last night. If I don't like what I hear, I'm going to sacrifice my nose in the name of my sister's honor."

Tony looked back at Mercy and raised his eyebrows in a questioning gesture. She managed to sigh, despite the large hand covering her mouth, then nodded. He slowly withdrew his hand. She shot him one more murderous look before speaking to her brother.

"Nothing happened on the stupid boat, Clark. Well, not 'nothing,' but not exactly 'something,' either."

Tony rolled his eyes heavenward.

"What is that supposed to mean?" Clark asked.

"That your nose is in no danger from Tony," Mercy said, her voice rising again. "But if you don't disappear from my sight in the next five seconds, I, personally, am going to take my best shot at your oh-so-precious beak. Got that, brother?"

"I think I'm outta here," Clark said.

"And so are you," Mercy said, poking Tony in the chest. "Go find someone else to play big macho brother with. You've maligned my womanhood, my femininity, and *your* nose is appearing very tempting as a target for my anger. Good night, sir."

"Now, Mercy, calm down," Tony said. "You're going to hyperventilate and—"

"Four seconds and counting."

"But what about the concert, the picnic supper?"

"I do not believe," she said stiffly, "that you wish to hear the words required to inform you as to what you can do with your band shell."

"Right," Tony said, nodding slowly. "I read you loud and clear."

"Good. Three seconds."

"Hell," Tony muttered, then spun on his heel and left the apartment.

Clark grabbed the edge of the door before it could close. "I guess you don't want to go out for pizza, huh?" he said.

"You have two seconds to—"

"'Bye," he said, and rushed out the door.

Mercy nodded decisively, then in the next instant became acutely aware of the heavy silence in the room. She walked slowly to the sofa and sat down, resting her elbows on her knees and cupping her chin in her hands.

So much for her beautiful night of ecstasy with Tony, she thought dismally. But he was so despicable. Saying she was absolutely safe when alone with him was really rude and demeaning.

Well, granted, no woman wanted to be in fear that her date was preparing to jump her bones at any given moment. But it was the way he had said "safe" that had hurt. It was as though last night had never really happened, and that there certainly would never be a repeat performance.

They had wanted each other on the *Perfection*. They had come so close. But then Tony had called a halt and . . . But tonight she had been going to . . . And now there was no tonight, and she was all alone. Missing Tony. Wanting Tony. Wishing Tony would storm back into her living room and demand that she quit acting like a witchy shrew.

But there was only silence.

She'd overreacted a bit, Mercy admitted. Her temper had gotten on a roll, and away she'd gone, yelling the roof down and banishing the knights from her castle.

What had she expected Tony to say to Clark? "I'm hot for your sister's body, so get out of here so I can tear off her clothes and get on with it"? Dumb. The man hadn't survived growing up in a rough neighborhood by making bold announcements that stood to get his face broken.

Mercy sighed.

She should have thrown Clark out first, she realized, then given Tony a chance to explain his damning "absolutely safe" statement. Had he reached the conclusion that he didn't want to make love with her? Or was he humoring a ridiculously old-fashioned big brother who was acting like a jerk?

Good questions, but it was rather difficult to get the answers when she'd tossed the man who had them out on his tush. So, now what? Darn it, she didn't know. She was alone, and lonely, and had never been so miserable in her entire life.

And with that depressing thought, Mercy burst into tears.

Tony and Clark rode down in the elevator without speaking. Each was lost in thought. In the middle of the lobby of the apartment building, they stopped and faced each other.

"Women," Clark said, "are extremely complicated creatures."

"Correction," Tony said. "Mercy Sloan is an extremely complicated creature. The women I know are all popped out of the same mold. I figured one of them out years ago, and had the key to the others that followed."

"No joke? That sounds great on the surface, Tony, but doesn't it get boring?"

Tony started to retort, then closed his mouth. He ran one hand over the back of his neck and nodded.

"Yes, now that you mention it," he said, "it really does."

"Well, I'll say this much for Mercy, she's been full of surprises since the day she was born. She had me, Drew, and Phil wrapped around her little finger the first time she smiled her toothless, gummy smile at us." He laughed softly as he pulled memory after memory from dusty corners of his mind. "Our folks said they'd have to make an appointment to play with Mercy because the brothers Sloan thought she was their personal property. We . . . well, we just love her a helluva lot, you know what I mean, Tony?"

A sudden and painful sensation gripped Tony's throat. No, he thought, he didn't understand the kind of love that Clark was talking about. It was an elusive entity that had always belonged to people other than Tony Murretti.

But the way Clark described it, it sounded like a treasure, a special gift that should be cherished. He envisioned it as being warm and comforting, capable of chasing away the chill of loneliness and the fears of unknowns that lurked in dark shadows.

"I'm glad," he said, his voice unnaturally

hoarse, "that Mercy grew up in a family like yours, that you're all still there for her. That's nice, Clark, really nice."

"Yeah, but at the moment I don't think Mercy feels that way." He shuddered. "That is one ticked-off pint-size package of dynamite."

"True."

"Tony, what did we do wrong upstairs? Hell, I was putting my handsome nose on the line for Mercy, and I got thrown out of her apartment for my noble deed. And you? She totally lost me there. She bounced you, too, and for the life of me I can't figure out how you screwed up."

"Damned if I know," Tony said. "Like I said, she's an extremely complicated woman."

And absolutely sensational, he added silently. She'd taken on two big men who each outweighed her by a hundred pounds, and sent them packing. With her dark eyes flashing, her cheeks flushed, her breasts rising and falling seductively with the exertion of her fury, she had been incredibly beautiful. He'd wanted to haul her into his arms and kiss her until her intense anger was channeled into desire for him. Only him. *Dammit, only him.*

"I, for one," Clark said, snapping Tony back to reality, "am staying out of Miss Mercy Sloan's way until she cools off. Then, if I'm brave enough, I'll ask her what set her off. Maybe. I have a feeling I won't become that courageous. Do you want to go get some pizza, Tony?"

Tony nodded. "Yes, pizza is fine. No, wait. I have a picnic in my car. Gourmet food from Daffodils and Daisies. No sense in letting it go to waste."

"Daffodils and Daisies? I've heard about that place. Phil's bought some food there, because with his wife just about to deliver, she hasn't felt like cooking. He told me the few times he's been in there, the place has been packed."

Tony nodded. "I'm not surprised. It's an excellent concept—take-out food that's nutritionally sound and even tastes good. The perfect answer for working mothers who are too busy to cook every night, and bachelors like me who can't cook. For a new business, they're doing exceptionally well."

"You sure know a lot about the place, Tony."

"Mmm."

Clark grinned. "You wouldn't happen to be a backer for Daffodils and Daisies, would you?

Tony whopped Clark on the back. "Come on, I'm starving. Let's eat the gourmet delights I have out there, drink the wine, and see if any clue reaches our then refueled brains regarding what in the hell we did to light a fuse under your sister."

"You're on. My place? It's only a few blocks from here."

"Fine."

At the lobby entrance, Tony stopped to look

back at the bank of elevators, then left the building, frowning.

Several hours later, Tony and Clark were slouched at opposite ends of Clark's deep-cushioned sofa. Five empty wine bottles were lined up along the mahogany coffee table in front of them. Clark had produced the additional four bottles after they had polished off the one included in the hamper from Daffodils and Daisies.

"The room's spinnin'," Clark said.

"Yep," Tony said.

"I'm drunk."

"Yep."

"Haven't been drunk for years and years."

"Yep. I'm drunk too."

"Why are we drunk?"

"I don't know." Tony thought about it for a minute. "Oh, Mercy. I'm drunk 'cause of Mercy."

"Yeah?"

"Yeah."

"Mercy's really ticked off at us. She's gotta temper, my baby sister. How come she threw us out?"

"Dunno."

"Me neither."

Tony sighed. "Mercy is so beautiful, Clark.

She's drivin' me nuts. I keep thinkin' about her, dreamin' about her."

"That's nice."

"No, it isn't. Neither is being drunk. I never get drunk 'cause I like to be in control, keep things perfect. Must be perfect. But I can't control Mercy."

"Me neither."

"Somethin' not right about the PTA, Clark."

"Huh?"

"My instincts are tellin' me something's wrong. I gotta figure it out. I gotta."

"Huh?"

"Aren't you listenin' to me?"

"I think so, but I'm too drunk to understand. 'Night, Tony. I have to go now."

Moments later, Clark was asleep, snoring loudly with his head resting on the top of the sofa. Tony looked over at him, blinked, then frowned.

"Hell," he said to the row of wine bottles. "No one to talk to about Mercy now. Mercy, Mercy, Mercy. What am I goin' to do about Mercy? I want her so damn much, but . . . Mercy says no PTA now, but I don't know. I don't . . ."

Tony tilted precariously to the left, attempted to straighten, failed, and fell asleep.

Seven

Early Monday morning, Tony was pulled from a deep, dreamless sleep by a rumbling noise. His foggy mind decided the noise was being produced by an engine that was probably attached to a piece of heavy machinery.

Oh, Lord, he thought, dragging the pillow over his head. He'd already awakened once that morning, feeling as though he'd been run down by a train. Now a dump truck, or whatever, was waiting to cream him? How long was he going to pay for his uncharacteristic drinking spree with Clark Sloan?

No, that didn't make sense, he mused, as more cobwebs of sleep faded. He'd been hit by the train *yesterday* when he'd surfaced from his stupor at Clark's apartment. He'd ached from head to toe, especially his head, but had managed to drive home and collapse on his bed.

The entire day had been wasted. He'd slept, taken aspirins, slept, carefully fixed a sandwich, and slept. This, he decided, had to be Monday morning. A gruesome hangover didn't last this long. So why was there a noisy dump truck getting ready to attack him?

He flipped the pillow aside and sat up, taking an inventory of his physical condition. He felt fine. It was a little after seven A.M., and there was definitely a piece of heavy equipment being operated close to his house.

He left the bed and strode naked to the window, brushing back the curtain to look at the area below.

There it was, a big yellow machine that was chomping at his weed-filled front yard. Several men were milling around, and smack-dab in the middle of the noisy confusion was Mercy Sloan.

He stared at Mercy for a long moment, then headed for the bathroom. A short time later he stood beneath the stinging spray of a hot shower.

He remembered now, he thought, as he lathered with soap. Mercy had told him that a crew would be clearing his property of weeds and debris.

He was also remembering with painful clarity the fiasco of Saturday night. It had begun with

Mercy tossing him and Clark out of her apartment, and had culminated in five bottles of wine and the hangover of the century. And he still didn't know what he'd done wrong.

After his shower Tony dressed in a summerweight suit and went downstairs. In the kitchen, the aroma of coffee greeted him, the automatic timer on the machine having clicked on to produce the lifesaving brew. With mug in hand, he walked into the living room to look out the front window.

Good morning, Mercy, he said silently. She was wearing those formfitting jeans again, and heat was rocketing through his body again. Her bright yellow top outshone the sun, and her auburn hair glowed like fire.

What in heaven's name was he going to do about her? How long could he possibly wait until he dragged her off to his cave and made love to her until they were both too exhausted to move?

A more immediate question, though, was whether she was still as mad as hell at him. There was only one way to find out the answer to that one.

He drained his mug and set it on an end table, then walked out the front door. The noise level trebled, and he saw a curtain of dust wavering through the air.

"Mercy," he called.

She was about twenty feet away, her back to

him, and didn't move when he shouted her name.

Hell, he thought, walking toward her. That machine was so loud, she wouldn't know if he dropped a bomb beside her.

He stopped directly behind her and tapped her on the shoulder. She turned, a questioning expression on her face, then her eyes widened when she saw him. He jerked his head toward the house, then turned and walked quickly back in that direction.

Mercy followed more slowly. She tried to tell herself it was because she was enjoying the view of his magnificent body clothed in yet another tailored suit. The truth was, she was still embarrassed by her behavior Saturday night, and she really didn't want to hear Tony tell her what a ninny she'd been.

She stepped into the house, and Tony closed the door. His face was masklike, and she had no idea what he was feeling.

"Coffee?" he asked.

"No, thank you."

"Would you like to sit down?"

"No, thank you."

He pushed his jacket back and planted his hands on his hips, and Mercy rolled her eyes. There was another one of those ultramasculine poses, she thought. She was not, however, going to yell at him about the way he stood in his own entryway. She was not, in fact, going to yell about anything. What she was working up the courage to do was to apologize for what happened Saturday night.

Her long, lonely, miserable Sunday seemed like punishment enough, but it wouldn't clean the slate. If only she could gauge Tony's mood, his frame of mind. Her body was certainly aware of her proximity to him, but that didn't tell her what he was thinking. Well, she'd just have to jump in.

"So," she said, "how's life?"

"How's life?" he repeated thoughtfully. "It's interesting at the moment. Confusing as hell, but definitely interesting."

"Oh. That's nice. I guess. Look, Tony, I'm sorry about the way I behaved Saturday night."

"You are?"

"Not that I didn't have just cause to be angry, you understand, but I overdid it a tad. Well, more than a tad. A lot, actually. Anyway, I apologize. Okay? End of story?"

"No."

"Blast. Why not?"

"Don't misinterpret my negative response, Mercy. I admire anyone who admits that they were out of line, made a mistake, an error, a—"

"All right, I get the message."

"But in this particular case, it's not enough. I want you to spell it out, explain exactly what you were so angry about. I've been over that scene in my mind a dozen times, and I can't figure out what

I, in your estimation, did wrong. Would you care to elaborate?"

"Oh, not really," she said breezily, "but thanks for the offer. I'd better go check on the yard crew."

Tony crossed his arms over his chest. "Let me rephrase that. Mercy, the next words out of your mouth will be the explanation as to why you ordered me out of your apartment on Saturday night."

She burst into laughter. "You sound like Perry Mason." Her smile disappeared as Tony narrowed his eyes. "Sorry," she mumbled.

"I'm waiting."

She sighed. "Well, you see, Tony, it's like this. Clark was in his old-fashioned, big-brother mode and . . . Actually, Clark is old-fashioned ninety-nine percent of the time, and—"

"Mercy," Tony said, a warning tone to his voice.

"Right. This is where it gets complicated. No woman wants to think she's in danger when she's with a particular man. But on the other hand, the way you said"—she made her voice as deep as possible—"'Mercy is absolutely safe with me'"—she coughed and resumed speaking in a normal voice—"made you sound as though you'd become a member of the Old-Fashioned Big Brother Club."

Tony nodded, but didn't speak.

"I was insulted, Mr. Murretti," she said, lifting

her chin. "I'm *not* your little sister. I'm a woman, I control my own life, am in charge of my own destiny. I'd chosen to make love with you that night, not to be tucked in and read a story. I had every right to be angry, and acted accordingly. A bit extreme, yes, but basically justified. There. You have your explanation."

He ran one hand over his chin. "I see. You had every intention of making love with me Saturday night. Was I to have any say in the matter?"

"Well, of course, silly man. I wasn't going to throw you onto the bed and tear your clothes off."

He chuckled. "Fascinating thought."

"I was under the impression—from previous encounters—that you desired me. After what you said Saturday night, I'm not so sure you do."

"Damned if I do and damned if I don't," he muttered.

"Pardon me?"

"Nothing. All right, Mercy, I get your point. You probably said all that Saturday, but it's hard to understand someone when they're shrieking loud enough to crack the plaster."

"Yes, well, I apologized for overreacting."

"Your apology is accepted, and I sincerely extend my own for insulting you, because that certainly wasn't my intention."

"Thank you."

"So? Does that clear the air?" he asked.

"I'd say so."

"Would you like to have dinner on the *Perfection* tonight?"

Oh, good Lord, Mercy thought. A whole evening on that bobbing-bed boat? Just the two of them? No neighbors, no telephone calls, no interruptions. How terrifying. Now, Mercy, calm down. This was exactly what she wanted. Remember?

"Mercy?"

"I'd be delighted, Tony."

"I'll pick you up at seven. Dress comfortably, and bring your bathing suit."

"Fine. Now, I really must go check on the yard crew and see how things are progressing out there."

Tony held up one hand. "First things first, Miss Sloan. We have yet to say a proper hello this morning, and now are due for a proper good-bye, as I'm leaving for the office." He stepped closer to her and rested his hands at her waist.

"Proper?" she asked, a funny squeak in her voice.

"Certainly." He lowered his head slowly, very slowly. Mercy's knees began to tremble, and her heart raced. "You do subscribe to the policy of doing things properly, don't you?" He flicked his tongue over her lips. She shivered. "With a goal of perfection?"

"Oh. Well. You bet." She raised her arms to encircle his neck. "Absolutely."

"Good."

The kiss was a shattering explosion of sensations. Their lips, their tongues, their bodies, met. Heat wove around them, swirled within them. Tony groaned as Mercy purred. His body ached with the desire he'd been suppressing for days, and only the thought of the men outside stopped him from sweeping her off her feet and carrying her to his bedroom.

He released her, reluctantly. "Office," he said in a hoarse whisper.

"Who?" she asked dreamily.

He cleared his throat and gently pulled her arms from his neck. "Shouldn't you be supervising my weeds?" he asked.

"Oh, goodness, yes," she said, stepping backward. "I'll—I'll see you at seven, Tony."

"Yes."

Neither moved, however. They continued to gaze into each other's eyes, eyes still hazy with passion. The distant noise of the machine outside was smothered by the sound of their quick breaths and the blood racing through their bodies.

It was Mercy who finally broke the magical spell.

"Seven o'clock," she said. "'Bye, Tony." She slipped around him and nearly ran out of the house.

"Until later, Mercy," he murmured.

Until later . . . What was going to happen "later," he wondered, on the *Perfection?* Dammit, she was coming at him from every direction, insisting that she wanted to make love with him and that she expected no commitment from him.

Why couldn't he just go along with her? he asked himself. He was sick to death of his noble, protective actions with her. He wanted Mercy, she wanted him. So be it. If his inner voice wouldn't shut the hell up, then he'd simply ignore it. Tonight Mercy Sloan would be his.

It was understandable, Mercy told herself during her lunch break, that all morning her thoughts had been focused on Tony. She was, after all, supervising the work at his home.

It also made sense that her mind continually skittered forward in time to the evening ahead, creating scandalous scenarios involving her and Tony and not many clothes. Tony Murretti had become very important to her, very quickly.

If only she hadn't lied. That lie was taking on enormous proportions, and she sensed it lurking in the shadows, ready to leap out and reveal itself, ending her precious time with Tony.

"Hey, Mercy!" a man yelled. "We're ready to start on the rear area."

"Okay," she hollered back. "Let's do it. Gobble

up those nasty weeds, guys. This place has to be absolutely perfect."

Just before seven that evening, Mercy placed a canvas tote bag on the sofa, then sank down next to it.

She was exhausted. She'd been on her feet the entire day, and had arrived home at six, hot and dirty. A shower, shampoo, and fresh clothes had helped immensely, but she could still feel fatigue deep in her weary bones.

Crawling into her bed and sleeping until morning sounded divine. On the other hand, the prospect of the evening ahead with Tony evoked far, far better images.

Her feelings for Tony were growing with each passing day, hour, minute. What she was doing was foolish, dangerous even, but she didn't care. She'd eventually cry, but for now . . .

A knock sounded at the door. She pushed herself up off the sofa and crossed the room.

"Hello, Tony," she said as she opened the door. "Come in."

"Good evening, ma'am," he said, stepping inside. She closed the door, and he immediately pulled her into his arms. "A very good evening, Miss Mercy Sloan."

He kissed her, and Mercy sighed with pleasure. The ecstasy of being with Tony surrounded her, and time lost meaning. When

Tony finally raised his head, they both drew in a much-needed breath of air.

"Ready to go?" he asked. "Do you have your bathing suit?"

"Yes, and yes."

He stepped back, his gaze sweeping over her. She looked very nautical in blue shorts and a blue-and-white top. "Nice outfit," he said, then grinned. "And great legs. You look dressed for a boat, and I just happen to have the boat."

"How convenient," she said, laughing as she retrieved her tote bag from the sofa. "All set." Tony Murretti didn't look too shabby himself. The khaki slacks and brown knit shirt accentuated his olive complexion and black hair. "The *Perfection* awaits, Captain."

They chatted comfortably during the drive to the marina. Tony complimented Mercy on the amount of work accomplished at his house that day. She praised the crew responsible.

They discussed the weather and a best-selling novel they both had read. Tony said the book was ridiculous. Mercy said it was wonderful, and that she'd wept her way through all the sad scenes.

"You actually cried?" Tony said. "It was fiction, make-believe. It wasn't as though those people really existed."

"While I was reading the book they existed," she said. "I cared about them, what was happening to them. The same holds true when I'm watching a good movie. I'd lose the pleasure if I kept telling myself it was all pretend."

"I can't see draining myself emotionally over fiction. Reality can be tough enough to deal with." He stopped at a red light and looked over at her. "I don't go to movies, and I usually read nonfiction, history, biographies, things like that. I read that best-seller just to see what the hoopla was all about." The light turned green, and he redirected his attention to his driving.

"You don't enjoy fiction at all?"

"Rarely," he said, shaking his head. "It frustrates me because the writer had the power to make everything perfect for the characters, and the majority of the time chooses not to."

"Perfect," she repeated. "You really do have a thing about perfection."

"Yes, I do. The goal to achieve perfection in all areas of my life has held me in good stead."

"But, Tony, such high standards could mean you're missing out on pleasures simply because they don't qualify, don't achieve your level of perfection. Don't you ever think about what's passing you by unnoticed?"

"No. Take us, for example. We're in *perfect* accord as far as our attitudes about relationships go. Right? Because we're in tune, we're together. Had my first impression of you been correct, I would have bowed out, but then I couldn't have missed what I never really had. Understand?"

"Yes," Mercy said, feeling a knot form and tighten in her stomach. "I understand."

"We *are* in agreement on the subject of our relationship, aren't we?"

"Yes. Of course. I told you that."

"Fine." Then why didn't he *feel* fine? Tony wondered. Why did he feel a sense of emptiness instead of relief as she told him what he wanted to hear? He'd needed her to say it one more time, and she'd done that, but . . . Damn, this was crazy. Anger was beginning to churn within him as he pulled up to the gate of the marina.

Was she nervous? Mercy asked herself as Tony went through the card ritual with the guard. Or was she calm, cool, and collected? She really didn't know because her fatigue was still dragging her down. She'd get a second wind once she'd had a swim and something to eat. She'd certainly better perk up, or she'd be dull as a doorknob rather than an interesting, intelligent companion for the evening.

The evening, she mentally repeated, that would include making love with Tony. The evening that would mean living her lie instead of just saying it. The evening that she had promised herself she would never regret.

More than an hour later, Mercy jerked awake as Tony cut the engines of the *Perfection*. She blinked, unsure for a moment where she was, then inwardly groaned in embarrassment as she realized she'd fallen asleep.

Once aboard the boat, Tony had announced that they'd motor to a secluded cove he'd discovered one lazy Sunday when he'd explored the area with the cabin cruiser. They'd left the marina and headed out, the running board lights on the *Perfection* glowing as darkness fell.

The water had been smooth as glass, and within minutes of curling up in a marshmallow-soft deck chair, Mercy had fallen asleep.

"The anchor is down," Tony said as he walked toward her. "Did you have a nice nap?"

"Yes, I did, but it was very impolite of me. You must have felt like a taxi driver with a dead-to-the-world passenger. I'm sorry."

"Hey, no problem. You were obviously beat, and as I thought about the day you'd put in at my house, I can see why. Are you feeling better now?"

"I think so, but I'm still rather foggy."

"The best remedy for that is a swim." He extended a hand to her. "Are you game?"

"Absolutely." She placed her hand in his, and he assisted her out of the low-slung chair. She glanced around. "It's so quiet here, so peaceful. I can't clearly see what the shore looks like, but aren't the stars beautiful?"

"They're perfect," he said, dropping her hand and wrapping his arms around her.

She encircled his waist with her arms and smiled up at him.

"I suppose," she said, "now that I know your stand on fiction, that you have no use for the legend of how Santa Barbara came to be."

He laughed. "Try me."

"Well, you see, once upon a time, years and years ago, the Chumash Indians lived on the offshore islands. One day after a soft summer shower, a rainbow appeared in the sky. Intrigued, the Indians climbed the rainbow to discover where it led."

"Nosy people," Tony said.

"Intelligently curious."

"Okay. Then what happened?"

"Those who made it safely to the end of the rainbow found what is now Santa Barbara. But . . ."

"But?"

"The Indians who slipped and fell off the rainbow into the ocean became . . . ta-da! . . . dolphins."

"Well, I'll be damned. So that's where dolphins came from."

"You believe the legend, of course."

"Mercy," he said, lowering his head toward hers, "I believe every word you've ever said to me."

He *had* to say that, she thought, feeling the now familiar knot tighten in her stomach. Maybe she should—

All thought fled Mercy's mind as Tony's lips met hers. The gentle kiss quickly deepened, and Mercy matched Tony's ardor. He nestled her to his body, his hard arousal pressing against her. The searing kissing went on and on beneath the millions of sparkling, diamondlike stars in the sky.

Slowly, reluctantly, Tony lifted his head.

"Let's go for that swim," he said. "You can change in the stateroom, and I'll meet you back up here."

Mercy nodded, unable to speak. The passionate kiss had seemingly used up her last ounce of air. On legs that were rather wobbly, she made her way below.

The decor in the stateroom matched the main area, with a royal blue spread on the double bed, gleaming mahogany furniture, and an easy chair upholstered in pale blue-and-white-striped fabric.

Mercy, however, hardly noticed anything except the bed. Her cheeks, still flushed from Tony's searing kiss, burned even hotter as her imagination quickly conjured up sensual images of what could happen in that bed.

"Oh my Lord," she murmured, placing one hand over her racing heart. "Shame on you, Mercy Sloan." She paused. "Correct that. Go for it, Mercy Sloan."

She changed into her pale green bikini, folded her clothes neatly on the chair, picked up her beach towel, and left the room. She stopped at the doorway to glance once more at the bed, then continued on. As she stepped back onto the deck, she came to a complete halt, the breath whooshing out of her.

Tony Murretti in a skimpy white bathing suit was truly the most incredibly beautiful sight she'd ever seen.

He was standing with his legs slightly apart and his hands splayed on his narrow hips as he gazed up at the sky. The starlight was nearly as bright as day, and Mercy could clearly see, and carefully scrutinize, every glorious inch of him.

His well-muscled arms complemented his wide shoulders. His chest was covered in dark, curly hair, and his legs were solid and strong. The white suit seemed to glow against his dark skin.

An ache gripped Mercy's throat, and unexpected, unexplained tears burned her eyes. With her gaze riveted on Tony, she was unable to move, or speak, or hardly breathe. Emotions tumbled through her like a raging river, until one broke free and touched her soul.

At that moment Mercy knew she was in love with Tony Murretti.

Oh, no, she thought frantically. This was all wrong. She wasn't supposed to fall in love with him. Yet even as she tried to deny it, the love seemed to swell within her, banishing all her fears and confusion.

Love was never wrong, she realized. It was only wrong when love was not given freely. No matter what the future brought for her and Tony, this night was still theirs to share.

She would live her lie and make love with Tony Murretti. He would never know that he had shared that intimate act with a woman who was deeply in love with him.

Mercy took a deep breath, lifted her chin, and walked across the deck to Tony.

"Making wishes on stars?" she asked.

Tony turned to look at her. "No, I . . ." He stopped speaking as his gaze skimmed over Mercy's body, barely covered by a green bikini. Her waist was even tinier than he'd thought, and the curve of her hips was made for his hands. Her skin seemed to gleam like satin in the silvery light, and he longed to touch and kiss every inch of it.

"You're lovely," he said, his voice low. "Absolutely exquisite. You look like a gift from the sea, from King Neptune's treasure room. God, Mercy, you're incredibly beautiful."

"Thank you," she whispered. "You're beautiful, too, Tony. You're the most magnificent man I've ever seen." She looked up at the heavens, then smiled at him. "There's a magic aura to this night, our night. The stars are shining just for us, because there's no one else in this special world. It was created for just the two of us."

He nodded. "Magic. I wonder . . . are there rules to magic? Yes, surely there are. You said 'just the two of us,' and that's how it must be. The royal decree from King Neptune is that there will be no magic in this place unless we're together."

Mercy nodded, unable to speak past the tightness in her throat. Her heart felt like it was going to burst with love for Tony Murretti. The man who believed that novels and movies were of little use, was indulging in a whimsical scenario with her of King Neptune, and magic, and a make-believe world created for them.

He extended one hand to her.

"Shall we visit the rest of our kingdom?" he asked.

She dropped her towel and placed one hand in his.

"Together?" she asked, looking directly into his dark eyes.

"It's the only way we'll be allowed to enter."

They stepped up on the padded bench at the edge of the deck, then balanced on the railing. Smiling at each other, they dove into the water. Their dives were perfectly synchronized, having the grace and elegance of majestic dolphins.

Eight

The water was clear, cool, and refreshing. Both Mercy and Tony were strong swimmers, and they raced around the *Perfection*. Tony won, but not by much. They held on to the ladder attached to the side of the boat while they caught their breath.

"You're quite a swimmer," Tony said.

"That comes from having three big brothers. I wanted to do everything they did, and do it as well. That, of course, didn't always happen, but I gave it my best shot."

"Good for you. I've only met Clark, and he's certainly devoted to you."

"We're a close-knit family. Clark and Drew are single, but Phil is married and will become a daddy in a few weeks. My parents will be back from their cruise in time for the arrival of their first grandchild. They're very excited about the baby. Well, we all are." She laughed. "Someone had better produce grandchild number two fairly quickly, or Julie and Phil's baby is going to be spoiled rotten by all of us."

Tony smiled. "I can well imagine." His smile slowly faded. "So, who do you think is the most favorable candidate to produce grandchild number two?"

Me, me, me, Mercy nearly yelled. She'd gladly volunteer. Oh, yes, she yearned for a child, but she wanted the baby's father to be Tony Murretti. And that would probably never happen.

She shrugged and forced a lightness to her voice. "I don't know. Clark is convinced there's an old-fashioned 'girl,' to quote, out there somewhere waiting for him to find her. He wants to raise his children the way we grew up, with a mother who stays home, has milk and cookies waiting after school, the whole nine yards. So far, he's not having any luck in his hunting campaign."

"I wouldn't think so. That's a pretty tall order to fill these days. What about Drew?"

"Well, he has no problem with a wife who has a career. It's his leisure-time activities that are holding up his marriage show. He's into all sorts of outdoorsy things. You know, camping, hiking, climbing mountains. Last year he rode the rapids of the Colorado River on a raft. He wants a wife who will share all that with him. So far he hasn't found her."

"And you, Mercy?" Tony asked quietly. "What are you looking for?"

She wasn't looking anymore, she thought. She was a foot away from the man she wanted, gazing at his beautiful face. She didn't have the emotional fortitude to bluff her way through the remainder of this conversation. Not right now.

"I'm not looking," she said. "Let's swim. I'm getting chilled staying in one place." She pushed away from the ladder and began to swim toward the front of the boat. "Coming?" she called back to him.

"In a minute."

"Grandchild number two," Tony repeated as he watched her swim away. It was so easy to visualize Mercy holding a tiny baby in her arms. She'd make a wonderful mother, and her home would overflow with sunshine and laughter.

Would she have a girl or a boy? A girl, he decided. A miniature Mercy, with curly auburn hair and a sweet face. Yes, a daughter. He'd like that. He'd walk in the door after a long day's work and immediately forget the hassle and stress of business as he was welcomed by Mercy and their baby girl. He'd gather them into his arms and—

Tony stiffened so suddenly, he lost his grip on the ladder and sank far enough to swallow a mouthful of water. He grabbed the ladder again as he sputtered and coughed.

Good Lord, he thought. He'd been in the water too long. His brain had shriveled. He never entertained ideas of marriage and babies. Hell, next thing he knew he'd be envisioning himself at a PTA meeting.

Damn that Mercy Sloan, she was working her magic on him again. It was fine with him if she had grandchild number two, providing he wasn't the father. No way. Some other man could . . .

"Oh, hell," he muttered.

The mental image of another man making love to Mercy was like a knife twisting in his gut. *Mercy Sloan was his.*

With an earthy expletive, Tony pushed away from the ladder and swam after her. Blanking his mind, he concentrated on the mechanics of swimming. His arms sliced cleanly and powerfully through the water, and he swam swiftly, as though a shark were nipping at his heels.

On the opposite side of the boat, he found Mercy floating lazily on her back, her eyes closed. He tread water next to her.

"Sleeping?" he asked.

"Yes," she said, not opening her eyes. "This is nature's water bed. Wake me in a month."

"You'd be a prune by then."

"True." She reluctantly opened her eyes and allowed her legs to sink so that she was treading water in front of him. "I don't want to admit it, but I'm chilled through. I guess I'd better get out. I've enjoyed this so much, I hate to end it."

"That's no problem. We'll just make certain that we come again soon . . . and often."

That sounded wonderful, Mercy thought wistfully. Tony was making it clear that he intended to be with her a great deal. But for how long?

She turned away from him, and started swimming toward the ladder on the side of the *Perfection.*

Within minutes, they were both standing on the deck wrapped in enormous beach towels. Mercy was shivering, and her teeth began to chatter.

"It's a warm shower for you," Tony said. "Go, before you turn blue. I'll shower, too, then we'll eat. Okay?"

Mercy nodded and hurried below. Tony watched her go, a frown knitting his dark brows.

What would it be like to be part of a family like the Sloans? he wondered. What would . . . Christmas be like?

He could imagine them all gathered in front of a beautifully decorated tree. Beneath it would be mountains of gifts wrapped in festive paper and topped with shiny bows. The house would reverberate with the jubilant sound of laughter, and glow with the warmth of love.

Then later in *their* home, bathed in the rainbow colors of *their* Christmas tree, he and Mercy would exchange the special gifts they'd bought for each other.

And there, before a crackling fire, they would make love.

"Christmas," Tony said.

The sound of his own voice startled him out of his reverie, and he jerked, dropping the beach towel. It fell unnoticed onto the deck, forming a puddle of vibrant colors.

He glanced quickly around, irrationally worried that Mercy, or even someone else, might have seen the scenario that had run through his mind, might have heard the yearning in his voice as he said the word Christmas.

He was shaken to the core, his breathing labored, his heart beating heavily. He was losing control of everything, his body *and* his emotions, and he was furious with himself *and* Mercy. He had to regain control, set the pieces of his life back in place to create his perfect world. That a woman he'd just met could unravel what he'd spent years to establish was not acceptable.

Even more, it was frightening.

Control, Murretti, he told himself as he crossed the deck. Control.

Mercy dressed after her delightfully hot shower, then stood in front of the mirror to brush her towel-dried hair. She swept one hand across the steamy mirror to clear it.

That woman, she thought as she gazed at her reflection, was in love for the first time in her life. That woman had stepped over a line to a place she'd never been before. That woman was feeling the greatest joy, yet was also aware of the greatest sorrow, at the same confusing time.

She attempted a smile, but it failed. Sighing dejectedly, she began to brush her damp hair.

What number was this in a disastrous set of four? she wondered. Heavens, she didn't know. She couldn't even keep straight whether Tony was good or bad for her.

All that was clear was that she was deeply in love with Tony Murretti. And that, for now, was as much as her weary mind was capable of handling.

When she entered the main area of the boat, Tony was already there, dressed in clean clothes and busily emptying the contents of a wicker basket onto the mahogany table.

Mercy instructed her nerves to hang in there, and joined him at the table.

"Look at all these fancy goodies," she said. "I'm famished."

"It's all ready," he said, not looking at her. "The picnic Clark and I ate the other night was great, so I decided to get another one. Have a seat."

She sat and watched as he opened the wine and filled their glasses. He put plates, napkins, and silverware in place, then sat down next to her.

She stared at him, noting the tight set to his jaw. She could literally feel the tension emanating from him.

"Tony?" she said quietly.

"Hmmm?" He still didn't look at her.

"Is something wrong?"

"Crab salad," he said, picking up a container. "Great stuff." He held it toward her, yet refused to meet her gaze.

She took the dish and plunked it on the table.

"Green grapes, purple grapes," he said. "Want some grapes?"

"Tony, would you forget the grapes for a minute? I asked you if something was wrong. We had such fun while we were swimming, and now it seems as though you've undergone a complete mood change. You're so tense, I feel like I'm sitting beside a bomb that's going to detonate in five minutes. The atmosphere is not conducive to enjoying crab salad and green grapes."

Tony sighed and sank back in his chair, then squeezed the bridge of his nose. He gazed up at the ceiling for a long moment, then finally looked at her.

"You're right," he said. "I did switch moods on

you, and I apologize. Let's just forget it and eat dinner."

She shook her head. "No. Why won't you tell me what's wrong? If it's something that *I* did, then I have the right to know."

A frown knit his brows. She held his gaze, refusing to flinch under his intense scrutiny. Heavy silence joined the tension hovering in the air.

"You've done nothing wrong, Mercy," he said finally. "I'm the one who's messing up the program."

She folded her arms on top of the table and leaned toward him. "What do you mean?"

He started to speak, then hesitated, making it apparent to Mercy that he was carefully weighing his words before he spoke. She waited, aware of the increased tempo of her heart.

"Mercy," he said finally, "I've been honest with you from the beginning. I told you I want no part of love, marriage, any kind of serious commitment."

"Yes," she said, nodding.

"That's still true, all of it. The thing is, my mind keeps going off on these weird tangents, creating mental scenarios that are like scenes from a movie, depicting you, me, a baby . . . Hell, it's crazy, and it's driving *me* crazy. *I don't want any of that.* You don't want it, either. Not now, at least."

He cares, Mercy's heart sang. Tony Murretti

was sullen and frustrated and angry, and it was wonderful. He'd actually envisioned them together? With a baby? Yes, Tony, that was what she wanted too. Now, not somewhere in the distant future, but *right now.*

"So, you can see," he went on, "you've done nothing wrong. As for me, don't worry about what I just said because I'm taking myself in hand, regaining control. I'll be back on the proper track in a minute."

Not if she had anything to say or do about it, Mercy thought. Tony was running from his emotions. Because his childhood had been devoid of love, he refused to allow love to touch his life as a man.

But the caring was there, and properly nurtured it could flourish, grow, match the intensity of her love for him—*if* Tony didn't smother it.

It was time for action, Mercy decided. She might still end up with a broken heart and a lonely future, but she wasn't going down without a fight.

"Tony?" she said.

"Yes?"

"Would you pass the grapes, please?"

"Grapes? Lord, Mercy, don't you have anything to say about what I just told you?"

She shrugged. "Not really. You explained the situation and what has to be done about it very clearly. There's no doubt in my mind as to what the course of action should be. Grapes, please?"

He shoved the dish of fruit into her hand, glowering at her.

"Thank you," she said pleasantly. "Now, let's see here. Green or purple? Life is full of major decisions, isn't it? I think I'll just have some of each, and solve that little problem."

Over an hour later, Mercy was struggling to keep from bursting into laughter. The meal was, at long last, completed, and it had been the most ridiculous meal she'd ever shared with someone. She'd chattered like a magpie while consuming more than her share of the delicious food, and she'd completely ignored Tony's still grumpy mood.

She patted her lips with her napkin, then leaned back in her chair with a satisfied sigh.

"My compliments to the chef," she said. "That was delicious. We certainly didn't leave any crumbs. Every bowl is as empty as Mother Hubbard's cupboard."

"Who?" Tony asked.

"You know, from the nursery rhyme. It's rather depressing, actually, because there's no bone for her dog in the cupboard. Poor little puppy."

"I've never heard of it, but it doesn't sound as though I missed much."

"Tony, didn't they read stories and nursery rhymes to you in that home?"

"No, they didn't have time for things like that because they were always understaffed."

"That's a shame." She propped one elbow on the table, resting her chin in her hand. "When I become a mother, I want to have an old-fashioned rocking chair. When the baby is tiny, I'll sit there to nurse him, then rock him to sleep. Later, it will be our special place for stories. He'll sit on my lap and point his chubby little finger at the pictures in the book and—"

"Her," Tony interrupted.

"Pardon me?"

"You keep saying 'him,' but I see you with a—a baby girl . . . and—Ah, hell."

He lunged to his feet, hauled a startled and wide-eyed Mercy out of her chair, and kissed her.

Mercy's shock was instantly replaced by raging desire.

As he drew her close, she wrapped her arms around his neck, urging his mouth even harder onto hers, parting her lips to meet his questing tongue.

She pressed her soft body seductively to his long, hard length, feeling his arousal, rejoicing in the knowledge that he wanted her as much as she did him.

Dear heaven, how she loved this man.

And she needed to make love with him.

The heat churning within her, that liquid fire burning low in her trembling body, could only be quelled by Tony.

Tony drank of Mercy's sweet taste like a thirsty man. Pulling her even closer, he marveled anew at her softness and gentle curves, the way she fit so perfectly against him.

He wanted her. Dear God, how he wanted her. Nothing else mattered, not now. He'd ignore the puzzling emotions swirling within him, shove aside the mental movies of a home with Mercy, and a baby girl. He would concentrate only on the reality of finally joining his body with Mercy's. What they were about to share wasn't just sex. No, they were going to make love because—

Don't think, Murretti, he ordered himself. *Don't think, just feel. Shut out the world beyond and make love to beautiful Mercy.*

He lifted his head and looked down at her. She met his smoldering gaze, and her expressive eyes radiated the message of her desire.

"Mercy . . ." he started, his voice gritty with passion.

"I want you, Tony," she said softly. "I want to make love with you now. There are no tomorrows, nothing beyond this moment. This is ours." She kissed him. "Make love with me, Tony Murretti. Please."

Slowly, tantalizingly, she outlined the shape of his mouth with the tip of her tongue. With a groan rumbling deep in his chest, he lifted her into his arms and carried her into the stateroom. A small lamp cast a rosy glow over the bed. He set Mercy on her feet, then kissed her again.

It was a deep, hungry, urgent kiss that snapped the last thread of control, sweeping them away on the raging current of passion. Reason was lost, desire reigning supreme.

Tony tore his mouth from Mercy's. As their labored breathing echoed in the quiet room, they shed their clothes with shaking hands.

Naked at last, they tumbled onto the bed, eagerly reaching for each other, seeking and finding lips, tongues, as a body soft molded to a body hard.

It was a time of discovery. Their hands never stilled as they touched, caressed, explored the mysteries and delights of the only other person who existed in their private world.

Tony concentrated on Mercy's breasts, drawing the lush bounty of one into his mouth, his tongue bringing the nipple to a taut button. She sighed in pleasure, her eyes drifting closed as she savored the sweet ache of her ever-growing desire.

Tony's hand skimmed over her, igniting a heated path in its wake. He traced lazy circles on the flat plane of her stomach, then journeyed along the gentle slope of her hip to her thigh.

He shifted slightly, leaving her breast to seek the other one. As he suckled with a rhythmic pull, his hand found the heated, moist darkness of her femininity, and the maddening stroking of his fingers matched the tempo of his mouth on her breast.

"Oh, Tony," Mercy whispered. "Please, come to me. Now. Now, Tony."

His muscles quivering from forced restraint, Tony raised his head to meet her gaze. He moved over her and kissed her deeply, his manhood heavy against her, boldly announcing what was to come, what he would bring to her.

He watched her face as he slowly entered her, waiting for any sign, the slightest flicker of pain. She felt so small beneath him, so delicate, making him acutely aware of his own size and strength, and of what he was asking her body to receive.

Even through the haze of passion that clouded her mind, Mercy realized what Tony was doing, why he was moving so tentatively. She felt the muscles in his upper arms trembling as she gripped them, and knew his control was costing him dearly.

Her heart nearly burst with love at the knowledge that he was placing her pleasure and comfort first. But she wanted him, all of him, filling her, consuming her.

With a sudden thrust, she lifted her hips. Tony groaned in defeat as well as relief as he sank deeply into her, sheathing himself in the hot, moist tightness.

"Oh, Lord," he groaned. "You feel so good. So good."

He began to move, slowly stroking, and she moved with him, clutching his hips, their gazes locked. Then he quickened the tempo, thrusting faster, harder, deeper. . . .

She wrapped her legs around him, urging him on, wishing this euphoria would never end, even as she strove to reach the summit of their wondrous climb.

Aching need built within them, swirling in ever-tightening circles, centering, focusing on what they sought. Closer. Such sweet pain. Tighter. Hot flames licked throughout them. Closer still. Higher. Until there, just beyond reach . . . they hovered, poised, then fell into ecstasy.

"Tony!"

"Mercy . . . Mercy . . ."

He threw back his head as he thrust one last time, his release following hers by one beat of his racing heart. He collapsed against her, spent, sated, feeling the lingering spasms ripple through her.

Gathering his last ounce of energy, he moved off her, then settled close to her, their heads resting on the same pillow, one of his arms across her waist.

Mercy turned her head to look at him, their faces mere inches apart.

"Tony, that was . . . so incredibly beautiful." Her voice was hoarse with unshed tears.

"Yes, it was." He kissed her gently on the forehead.

It had been, he knew, like nothing he'd experienced before. The emotions he'd been determined to ignore had crept in, combining with the physical pleasure and seeming to touch his very soul. And instead of feeling anger at his loss of control, he was aware only of the glory, the ecstasy, of making love with Mercy.

Mercy snuggled closer to Tony, relishing the mere presence of his magnificent body.

Number three, she thought suddenly. She'd nearly forgotten. This was number three with Tony. And at least for tonight, there was no doubt in her mind that the Tony Three qualified as wonderful. Words had not been invented to describe their exquisite lovemaking.

What would be number four? she wondered, then she frowned. She knew what it was and for the first time ever, her series of four would not be completed.

Number four would be for Tony Murretti to fall in love with her, and declare that love.

And despite her early determination to nurture his seed of caring, Mercy knew that was never going to happen.

Nine

This, Mercy thought, must have been how Cinderella felt when midnight came and ended her glorious, fairy-tale night. In a word, miserable.

She sighed and watched the lights of Santa Barbara whiz by as Tony drove to her apartment.

She had just begun to drift off to sleep in the stateroom on the *Perfection* when he had whispered in her ear that it was getting late and tomorrow was a workday. Reality had landed in that bed with an extremely rude thud.

Now there they were, speeding along, preparing to go through the end-of-date ritual at her door. It was absurd, she decided. She loved this man. She wanted to tell him, and anyone else who would listen, that she was in love.

That, however, would be incredibly stupid. A declaration of that nature would get her nothing more than one last glimpse of Tony's nifty tush as he hightailed out of her life. She'd do well to shut off her mind before she thoroughly depressed herself.

All too soon, as far as Mercy was concerned, she was handing her key to Tony and he was unlocking her apartment door. At the moment he pushed the door open, the telephone rang.

"Who would be calling this late?" Mercy said, worriedly, rushing inside.

"Not all late-night calls are bad news," Tony said, following her into the apartment.

Mercy snatched up the receiver of the telephone. "Hello?"

"Mercy?"

"Drew? What's wrong? Why are you calling so late?"

"I've been trying to reach you for hours. You didn't even leave your answering machine turned on. Where have you been?"

"Forget that and tell me why you called."

"Julie is in labor. I'm at the hospital with Phil and Clark. We figured you'd want to be here."

"Julie is what? She can't do that. It's too soon."

"Tell it to the kid. The doctor told Phil that the baby is a good size and not to worry. Sure. Right. Phil is coming apart at the seams. Are you going to join this party?"

"Yes, of course I am. I'll leave right now."

"Where were you tonight?"

"'Bye, Drew." She hung up, then spun around to face Tony. "I hate to rush you off, but I've got to get to the hospital because Julie is having her baby."

He smiled. "Grandchild number one is on the way, huh?"

"Yes, and my folks are going to have a fit because they're not here. Well, we can't tell the baby to stay put until Grandma and Grandpa's cruise ship docks. I've got to get going. Where are my car keys? Oh, they're in your hand with the apartment key. That's nice. Oh, dear, I think I'm a wreck."

He nodded. "I'd say that's a fairly accurate assessment. Therefore, I'll drive you to the hospital."

"That isn't necessary. You said yourself that it's late and tomorrow is a workday."

"Mercy, I'm driving you to the hospital."

"Good idea. Let's go."

The waiting room on the maternity floor of the hospital looked, Tony decided, like a movie set. The only things missing were overflowing ashtrays and a haze of smoke.

Mercy quickly introduced Tony to Phil and Drew, then asked if there was any news of Julie.

"Of course not," Phil said. He paced across

the floor. "It's been years since they told me anything. She's being held for ransom. I should have checked the credentials of this place."

"Phil," Mercy said, "we were all born in this hospital."

"Big deal."

"Now I know where you were tonight," Drew said, gazing speculatively at Tony.

"Cool it, Drew," Clark said. "Your nose isn't as great looking as mine, but I don't think you want it broken."

"Huh?" Drew said.

"How's life, Tony?" Clark asked.

Tony grinned. "Interesting."

"Isn't that the truth?" Clark said. "You know, having a baby is hard on the nerves. I feel as though we've been here for a week."

"Years," Phil muttered, still pacing. "It's been years."

"Now, let's all calm down and sit down," Mercy said, attempting to sound like their mother. "Getting into a dither never solved a thing."

"If you're trying to imitate Mom," Drew said, "you're not cutting it."

She glared at him and sank onto a sofa. Tony settled next to her.

"So," Drew said, sitting in a straight-backed chair, "what fascinating social event did you two attend tonight?" He looked from Mercy to Tony, then back to Mercy.

"Don't push it, Drew," Clark said. He paused, then added, "Ah, hell, go ahead and push. Getting your busted nose patched up will give us something to do while we're waiting."

"Why are you harping about my nose?" Drew asked.

"Trust me," Clark said.

"Have you seen Julie at all?" Mercy asked Phil, as he passed in front of her.

"Yeah, about fifteen minutes ago," he said. "She patted my hand and told me to be brave."

Tony coughed to camouflage a burst of laughter. Mercy glanced at him and smiled. He took one of her hands in his, holding it on his thigh.

Drew's eyes widened. He opened his mouth to ask what was going on, but Clark forestalled him.

"Shut up, Drew." Clark looked at Tony. "How's the landscaping coming at your place?"

"Who cares?" Phil said, crossing between them. Everyone ignored him.

"If noise and dust mean anything," Tony said, "progress is being made."

"Don't you think," Drew said, "you were out rather late, Mercy, considering that you're in the middle of a big project?"

"Shut up, Drew," Clark said.

A nurse stepped into the room. "Mr. Sloan?"

"Yes?" three men answered in unison.

"The daddy Sloan," the nurse clarified.

"That's me," Phil said. "Me. Yes. That's who I

am. The father. What's wrong? Why are you asking for me? Don't try to spare me, just lay it on the line. No, forget that. Be kind. Break it to me gently. What's happened to my Julie?"

The nurse shook her head. "You are just about the worst nervous daddy I've seen and, believe me, I've seen some beauts."

"Does he get an award for worst?" Drew asked.

"Shut up, Drew," Phil said.

"Mr. Sloan," the nurse went on, "your wife is about to be taken into the delivery room. She said you were planning to witness the birth of your child, so you need to scrub and get your surgical greens on. However, considering the shape you're in, I'm not certain that's a good idea. We can't have you upsetting our little mother. She has a big job ahead of her."

"I'm fine, fine," Phil said quickly. "I promised Julie I'd be there. I've got my act together now. Really."

"Well," the nurse said, eyeing him warily, "we'll give it a try, but if you panic in there, we're tossing you out. Come on." She turned and left the room.

Phil didn't move.

"Phil," Tony said, "you're supposed to go with her."

"Oh." Phil hurried out of the waiting room.

Clark whistled. "I sure hope I don't come unglued like that when I'm going through this."

"*I* won't," Drew said. "Having a baby is a natural process. Those of us in tune with nature understand that. What about you, Tony? Do you think you could handle this bit?"

Tony frowned. "I've never given it any thought before, but . . . Well, it's got to be rough being stuck in a room like this, not knowing what's happening to the woman you love, except that she's in pain because she's having your baby. As much as I'd like to say I'm positive I'd stay calm and in control, I'm not that convinced that I would."

Oh, how she loved Tony Murretti, Mercy thought, her gaze riveted on his face. He could have taken a macho stand on the subject, or refused to give it any thought at all. But he'd truly thought about it and shared his innermost feelings.

And the best part of all, she mused, was that, whether he was aware of it or not, Tony's grip on her hand had tightened as he'd answered Drew's question.

Drew sank back in his chair. "I never looked at it quite like that before. Yeah, that's heavy, all right."

They all fell silent then, and time ticked slowly by.

About forty-five minutes later, everyone jerked in surprise when Phil came barreling into the room.

"It's a boy!" he yelled. "Julie had—we have a

boy. Six pounds, two ounces, even though he's early. Julie was sensational. It's a boy. He's red, and wrinkled, and screaming his head off, and he's . . . he's so beautiful."

They all rushed over to him, offering congratulations.

Mercy kissed Phil on the cheek. "What are you going to name him?"

"Phillip Frederick Sloan the Third. We'll call him Trey."

"Oh, Dad will be thrilled," Mercy said. "I wonder if you can get a telegram sent to their cruise ship?"

"Sure," Tony said. "It's done all the time."

"Excuse me," the now familiar nurse said. "Master Sloan is ready for viewing. Anyone interested? Then you are all going home. Our mother is asleep for the rest of the night."

They followed the nurse like obedient little soldiers. Near the end of the corridor, she pointed to a drape-covered window, then disappeared through a door. A few minutes later the curtain was whisked open and the nurse stepped forward. Nestled in the crook of her arm was a small bundle wrapped in a blue blanket.

"There he is," Phil said, beaming. "My son. Isn't he sensational?"

"You weren't kidding about the red and wrinkled," Drew said.

"Shut up, Drew," Mercy said.

"Hey," Drew defended himself, "I think he's a neat kid. He's got some hair there. Not a lot, but it's hair. I like his chin. He's got the Sloan chin."

"Somewhere on this planet," Clark said, his eyes glued to the baby, "is an old-fashioned girl who wants a half dozen of those little people, and is willing to stay home and tend to them."

"Hi, Trey," Phil said, waggling his fingers. "I'm your dad."

"He's so precious," Mercy said softly. "He's a miracle, Phil. A tiny miracle. You and Julie are very blessed and very lucky."

Tony stared down at Mercy, surprised by the wistful tone to her voice.

She looked up at him. "Trey *is* a miracle, and Julie and Phil *are* lucky because they were able to start their family when they decided the time was right." She averted her eyes from his. "Well, you already know where I stand on the issue."

"Yes," Tony said quietly. "You've made it very clear."

"'Bye, Trey," Phil said, as the nurse stepped back. "Remember, I'm your dad."

"See ya, kiddo," Clark said.

"Great chin," Drew said.

The curtain was closed, congratulations were once again issued to the proud father, then the group dispersed, everyone heading for different elevators, which would deposit them closest to the exit near their cars.

Phillip Frederick Sloan III slept blissfully on,

not knowing how many hearts he'd touched and won that night.

Two hours later, Mercy flopped onto her stomach, punched her pillow, and closed her eyes. Five seconds later, her eyes popped open again. Moaning, she rolled onto her back and stared up into the darkness.

Something was wrong with Tony, she thought for the umpteenth time. Before they'd even left the hospital, she'd sensed him putting an intangible distance between them. His walls were more solid, and more securely in place, than ever before.

Why?

The lovemaking they'd shared had been exquisitely beautiful. It had been a wondrous night, a night to be treasured and cherished.

No, she reasoned. It wasn't what had taken place on the *Perfection* that had caused the change in Tony. It was the baby. Something had happened when he'd stood there with all of them seeing the tiny miracle who was Phillip Frederick Sloan III.

But that didn't make sense. Even though images had flitted through her mind of a baby created by her and Tony, she'd said the right words. She'd emphasized that babies would not be a part of her life until much further down the road.

So what was wrong with Tony?

"Men," she said, wrinkling her nose.

She willed herself to get some sleep during the few remaining hours left to her before it was time to meet the landscaping crew at Tony's. She finally dozed, dreaming of dozens and dozens of happy, smiling babies.

Tony stood before his bedroom window, his hands braced high on the frame as he stared out unseeing at the night. He'd given up trying to sleep. He was too tense to relax.

And his mind? It was a mess, a jumble of fragmented images and thoughts. From the first glimpse he'd had of Phil's son, something had shifted within his own mind and heart, his very soul.

It was as though he'd been standing outside of himself, watching himself change into someone he didn't know. And yet, when he'd merged with himself again, he'd felt comfortable with who he now was, and had experienced a soothing rush of warmth.

He had looked at that baby and known without the faintest doubt that he, too, wanted a child. He, too, wanted a wife, a partner, the other half of who he was. He wanted to spend the rest of his life with Mercy Sloan.

Because he was deeply and forever in love with her.

He dragged both hands down his face. His heart was racing, and a trickle of cold sweat was running down his back. There was a knot in his gut, a metallic taste in his mouth, and a dreadful emotion burgeoning within him.

It's name was Fear.

Dear God, he thought, he couldn't handle this. He could not, would not, strip himself bare and vulnerable, place himself in a position where someone else, where Mercy, controlled his future happiness.

He was in charge of the life of Tony Murretti. He strove for and achieved perfection. He would spend the remainder of his days alone, by choice.

He crossed the room and stretched out on his bed. But as dawn crept over the horizon and announced the new day, he still had not slept.

Her hands on her hips, Mercy watched as black plastic was rolled across Tony's front yard. The ground already had been sprayed with weed-killing chemicals, and gravel would cover the plastic.

It was a process she'd supervised many times, and she could practically do it in her sleep. Due to the fact that she was exhausted from her restless night and her emotional turmoil, she was grateful she wasn't facing a challenging part of the project.

"Mercy."

She spun around at the sound of her name and saw Tony standing at his front door.

"Yes?" she said, searching his face for some clue as to his frame of mind. Nothing was evident in his expression.

"May I speak with you privately, please?"

No, she thought. She didn't want to hear what he had to say, because her instincts were telling her that a major and chilling change was about to take place in her life. Still, she'd have to talk with him sometime.

She entered the house with dragging steps and followed him to the entrance of the living room. He stopped halfway across the room and turned to face her. She lifted her chin and met his gaze directly.

"Mercy," he began, his voice oddly flat. "I feel it would be best if we didn't see each other again."

"Oh?" she said. "Why, Tony?"

"It's just the best thing to do."

"That's not good enough. I want to know why."

He dragged one hand through his neatly combed hair, tousling it.

"I suppose I do owe you an explanation, especially after . . . Well, after last night." He paused. "Look, I've admitted from the start that I don't behave true to form around you. I've told you things about myself that no one else knows,

I've felt emotions toward you that I've never felt with anyone."

A warm glow of hope slowly pushed aside the chill of anxiety within Mercy. She forced herself to maintain a blank expression on her face as she listened to Tony.

"You weave spells over me, Mercy," he went on, "with a magic I don't understand, nor welcome. I'm ending this relationship. I realize this is all very abrupt, but we did agree that it was a temporary affair."

He took a deep breath, then exhaled slowly. "I have to do this because . . ." He cleared his throat. ". . . because . . . Hell, because I do, that's all."

Because he loved her, Mercy thought joyfully. Tony Murretti had fallen in love with her. And he was scared to death. She loved it.

"Well, that's that then," she said. Until she came up with a new plan of action. "No hard feelings." No, they were soft, gentle feelings. Feelings of love. "I have one request, though, Tony."

"Which is?"

"I'd like to know about the Christmas tree."

"Damn." He stared up at the ceiling for a moment, then looked at her again. "Ah, hell, why not? What's one more totally out of character action on my part?"

She nodded.

"The first year I was at the home where my mother dumped me, I . . . worried that Santa

Claus wouldn't know where I was. Then three days before Christmas, a beat-up artificial tree suddenly appeared in the dining room. It was a piece of junk, but at the time I was thrilled because I figured Santa would find me because of that tree."

An achy sensation gripped Mercy's throat, and she could feel tears burning in her eyes.

"We all decorated that thing," he continued, "with paper and popcorn chains, and one short string of lights. I thought it was terrific. But then . . ."

He stopped speaking, and she saw pain flicker across his face before he regained control. She willed the tears brimming in her eyes not to spill over onto her cheeks.

"Then," he went on, "on Christmas Eve morning, some men came and took the tree away in a truck."

"Why?" she asked. "Why on earth would they do something like that?"

"The tree had been loaned to us. It actually belonged to a nursing home across town. We could use it, but the agreement was that it went to the other place on Christmas Eve."

"Oh, Tony," Mercy whispered. A single tear slid down one cheek, and she dashed it away.

"In the years that followed," he said, "we sometimes had a tree, sometimes not. I made myself not care one way or the other. But in my subconscious, I guess, it mattered. It mattered a helluva lot. I don't really remember how old I was when I vowed that someday I would have a Christmas tree of my very own that no one could ever take away."

He stared blindly out the window. "That tree wouldn't be just for Christmas. I wanted to be able to see it every day of my life, whenever I wished to. It would be tangible evidence that I was no longer, and would never be again, vulnerable to the whims of other people. And that's why, Mercy, I asked you to plant a Christmas tree in my yard, where I could see it every day for the rest of my life."

"I—I understand," she said, giving up her battle against her tears. "Thank you for telling me. I . . ." She stopped speaking as emotions choked off her words.

"I'm going away on business," he went on, still staring out the window. "I'll be in Europe for a while, so when you finish the work here, mail the bill to my office. Marianne will see that it's paid."

"Yes."

"So, I guess . . . that's all we have . . . to discuss. I wish you every happiness and . . . Good-bye, Mercy."

"Good-bye, Tony." She turned and hurried out of the house.

When Tony heard the front door close behind her, he shifted his gaze to where she had stood.

"I love you, Mercy Sloan," he said, "but I don't have the courage to ever, *ever*, tell you."

Ten

On a sunny afternoon three weeks later, Clark burst into the office of Sloan Nursery and Landscaping, causing Mercy, Drew, and Phil to jump in their chairs.

"I need this like a hole in my sock," Phil said. "I have a pounding headache from lack of sleep, thanks to that seven-pound air raid siren named Trey, and my brother roars into the building like a tornado."

Clark glared at Phil. "You have been a grouch ever since you became a father. That's a terrible example to be setting for my nephew."

"Stuff it," Phil said. He folded his arms on the top of his desk and dropped his head down on them.

"Was there a purpose for your entrance-with-obnoxious-flair?" Drew asked. "Or did it simply seem like a good idea at the time?"

"Oh," Clark said. "Hey! Listen up. I did it!"

"What? What?" Phil said, jerking upright. "I'll get him, Julie. It's my turn."

"Phil," Clark said, "you are *not* a well man."

"He's a tired man," Mercy said. "Okay, Clark, we'll humor you. What have you got?"

"What none of our other less-than-genius-level plans produced over the past three weeks," he said, appearing extremely pleased with himself.

Mercy felt the color drain from her face, and she sat up straighter in her chair.

"Tony?" she asked tentatively. "You've found out when Tony is coming back from Europe?"

"Yep," Clark said, his expression becoming even more smug.

"Please don't joke about this, Clark," Mercy said. "It's too important to me."

Clark immediately became serious, and sat down beside her.

"I'm not playing games with you, sweetheart," he said. "None of us are. When you sat us all down and told us you were in love with Tony Murretti, we respected the fact that this was serious. We haven't told Mom and Dad because they'd just worry about you. Hell, *I'm* worried about you, but I've done my part."

"How did you get the info?" Drew asked. "I bombed out with Tony's marine sergeant assis-

tant. One cannot charm a member of the ge-
stapo."

"I failed with her too," Phil said. "When I told
her I needed to know when Tony would be home
so I could schedule an inspection for termites,
she informed me to recheck my records, because it was inspected months ago."

"Calling and saying I had flowers to deliver to
Mr. Murretti got me nowhere," Mercy said. "I
was told to keep the flowers and forward the
card to his office as Mr. Murretti was out of the
country."

"Well, Mr. Murretti is finally due back," Clark
said. "Children, I went for sophistication in my
detective mode. I looked up a buddy of mine
who is a computer hack. This guy can tap into
any system he wants to. You don't want to know
what he has access to. He's a jail sentence
waiting to happen."

"And?" Mercy asked impatiently.

"He's been monitoring all incoming airline
flights from overseas for the past two and a half
weeks, and Tony is flying in today. Figuring the
time it'll take him to clear customs, remember
where he parked his car, and drive home, Tony
Murretti should arrive at his residence at ap-
proximately eight-twelve tonight."

"Oh, Lord," Mercy said, her hands flying to
her cheeks. "This is it."

"Only if you want it to be," Drew said. "Are
you really sure that you—"

"Yes," she interrupted. "I love him, Drew. This is my last and only chance. I know it's risky, and I could be making a terrible mistake, but I have to try. I can't be any more miserable than I've been for the past three weeks."

"You'd better get going," Phil said. "You have a lot to do."

"Do you want some help?" Clark asked.

"No. I'll do it myself. It's better this way. Listen, thank you, all of you. You're the best brothers in the world, and I love you." She took a deep breath. "Well, here I go."

None of her brothers spoke as she left the office. But after the door had swung closed behind her, the three men exchanged looks of great concern.

At 8:02 that night, Tony Murretti drove his sleek car along the street leading to his house.

He was exhausted, he thought. He had an enormous case of jet lag, combined with not having slept well for the past three weeks. He had not slept well because of Mercy Sloan. She had taken up permanent residency in his mind, and had haunted him day and night.

The hold she had on his heart was incredibly strong too. But his fear was stronger. He missed her and ached for her, wanted to see her, hold her, even just talk to her. More than that, though, he wanted to marry her and create a home with her. But that would never happen.

Besides, he told himself yet again, Mercy didn't love him. She wasn't remotely interested in a serious relationship. He was certain of that. On the day he'd ended it, she'd been completely nonchalant. She'd accepted his decision with a shrug and gone back outside to mess around in his yard.

Any way he looked at the situation, it was hopeless. Any way he looked at his future, the word 'lonely' echoed unmercifully in his mind.

Darkness had fallen when, at eight-twelve, Tony turned into his driveway. His headlights picked up the neat row of lilac bushes edging the driveway, and he glanced from side to side to see what else had been planted.

Suddenly his eyes widened, and he slammed on the brakes. He could make out the huge silhouette of his dark house and there, in front of it, was . . .

No, he thought, shaking his head. It *wasn't* there. He was so tired, he was imagining things. The brain could only take so much abuse, and his had blown a fuse.

He tentatively pressed on the gas pedal and inched the car forward, willing the mirage to disappear.

It didn't.

"Dammit," he muttered. "I don't have time to be crazy."

He stopped about twenty feet from the house and got out of the car, his gaze fixed on what he told himself wasn't there.

There was not, he thought as he walked forward, a beautifully decorated, rainbow-lights-aglow Christmas tree standing in sparkling splendor in front of his house.

He moved closer, and his heart skipped a beat.

And, no, he thought, Mercy Sloan was not sitting in a rocking chair beside the tree, wearing a long red robe and knitting something with pink yarn. That was absurd. She was the most beautiful creature he'd ever seen, *but she was not there.*

And there were not brightly wrapped gifts under the majestic tree, nor silver tinsel and delicate ornaments on its branches, and a star wasn't on the top, reaching toward the heavens.

None of this was real.

Was it?

"Mercy?" he whispered.

She lowered the knitting to her lap and smiled at him.

"Hello, Tony," she said softly. "Welcome home. Merry Christmas."

He narrowed his eyes. "You're a product of my jet lag. Right?"

"No."

"Oh, God." He rubbed his forehead. "You're really here."

"Yes."

"Why?"

Mercy stood up, setting the knitting on the rocker. She clasped her hands loosely in front of her and prayed her trembling legs would support her. The mere sight of Tony had caused tears to well in her eyes, and she willed herself not to cry before she'd said what was in her heart.

"Tony, I'm taking a tremendous risk with my pride and my heart by being here like this. But I feel that you, that what we have, is worth it. Tony Murretti, I love you. I want to spend the rest of my life with you as your wife and the mother of your children. I want to make a commitment to love you until death parts us. Not later, Tony, not someday, but now. Right now."

"But . . ."

"I wasn't truthful with you," she went on. "I led you to believe that a casual affair was fine with me, that I wasn't interested in more. That wasn't true, but I felt it was the only way to have more time with you, be with you, make love with you. Oh, my darling Tony, I love you so very much."

She smiled through her tears. "You want to know why I'm here tonight, why the Christmas tree is decorated? Because, Tony, having a Christmas tree every day of your life was your dream, and I want to share it with you. I believe . . ."

She took a deep breath and gathered the remainder of her courage, knowing that what she was about to say was going to determine her destiny.

"I believe that—that you are in love with me, that you love me with a love as deep, and rich, and real, as mine is for you. I believe that you want me and everything this beautiful tree represents, but that you're . . . afraid to love. You're frightened, Tony, and I understand that, and respect that."

"But, Tony?" she went on, a sob catching in her throat. "We could conquer your fear of loving if we did it together. We could have Christmas every day for the rest of our lives. I love you. And that's—that's all I have to say."

Silent seconds ticked by as Tony stared at Mercy, the rocker, her knitting, then up, up, the entire length of the glowing tree. When he spoke at last, his voice was rough with emotion.

"Mercy Sloan," he said, "this is the most difficult battle I have ever fought. I've never been so terrified in my life but . . . Oh, God, Mercy, I love you. I swear I do. I don't want to go through life without you, be alone and lonely because of my fears. I love you, I want you, and, dear Lord, I need you. Forever, Mercy. We'll have Christmas-tree days, and lovemaking nights and . . . Ah, Mercy, come here."

He opened his arms and she hurled herself into his embrace, wrapping her arms around his neck and burying her face against his shoulder. He held her tightly, as though he'd never let her go.

She finally raised her head and smiled at him. "Please say it again. Tell me you love me."

He smiled too. "I love you."

"Oh, Merry Christmas, number four."

"What?"

"I'll explain later. I want to make love with you, Tony. I missed you so much."

"Then let's go inside. Do you want to get your yarn so it won't get dusty?"

"No," she said, laughing. "I don't know how to knit."

They walked to the front door, then turned for one last look at the tree.

"Merry Christmas, my love," Mercy whispered to him.

"Merry Christmas."

They went inside the house and closed the door. The Christmas tree stood alone in majestic splendor, as though guarding their private world.

Through the night, Mercy and Tony made wondrous love, declaring their commitment to a lifetime together.

And with each passing hour, the star on the top of the Christmas tree glowed brighter and brighter.

THE EDITOR'S CORNER

What a marvelously exciting time we'll have next month, when we celebrate LOVESWEPT's ninth anniversary! It was in May 1983 that the first LOVESWEPTs were published, and here we are, still going strong, still as committed as ever to bringing you only the best in category romances. Several of the authors who wrote books for us that first year have become *New York Times* bestselling authors, and many more are on the verge of achieving that prestigious distinction. We are proud to have played a part in their accomplishments, and we will continue to bring you the stars of today—and tomorrow. Of course, none of this would be possible without you, our readers, so we thank you very much for your continued support and loyalty.

We have plenty of great things in store for you throughout the next twelve months, but for now, let the celebration begin with May's lineup of six absolutely terrific LOVESWEPTs, each with a special anniversary message for you from the authors themselves.

Leading the list is Doris Parmett with **UNFINISHED BUSINESS**, LOVESWEPT #540. And there is definitely unfinished business between Jim Davis and Marybeth Wynston. He lit the fuse of her desire in college but never understood how much she wanted independence. Now, years later, fate plays matchmaker and brings them together once more when his father and her mother start dating. Doris's talent really shines in this delightful tale of love between two couples.

In **CHILD BRIDE**, LOVESWEPT #541, Suzanne Forster creates her toughest, sexiest renegade hero yet. Modern-day bounty hunter Chase Beaudine rides the Wyoming badlands and catches his prey with a lightning whip. He's ready for anything—except Annie Wells, who claims they were wedded to each other five years ago when he was in South America on a rescue mission. To make him believe her, Annie will use the most daring—and passionate—

moves. This story sizzles with Suzanne's brand of stunning sensuality.

Once more Mary Kay McComas serves up a romance filled with emotion and fun—**SWEET DREAMIN' BABY,** LOVESWEPT #542. In the small town where Bryce LaSalle lives, newcomers always arouse curiosity. But when Ellis Johnson arrives, she arouses more than that in him. He tells himself he only wants to protect and care for the beautiful stranger who's obviously in trouble, but he soon finds he can do nothing less than love her forever. With her inimitable style, Mary Kay will have you giggling, sighing, even shedding a tear as you read this sure-to-please romance.

Please give a rousing welcome to newcomer Susan Connell and her first LOVESWEPT, **GLORY GIRL,** #543. In this marvelous novel, Evan Jamieson doesn't realize that his reclusive next-door neighbor for the summer is model Holly Hamilton, the unwilling subject of a racy poster for Glory Girl products. Evan only knows she's a mysterious beauty in hiding, one he's determined to lure out into the open—and into his arms. This love story will bring out the romantic in all of you and have you looking forward to Susan's next LOVESWEPT.

Joyce Anglin, who won a Waldenbooks award for First Time Author in a series, returns to LOVESWEPT with **OLD DEVIL MOON,** #544. Serious, goal-oriented Kendra Davis doesn't know the first thing about having fun, until she goes on her first vacation in years and meets dashing Mac O'Conner. Then there's magic in the air as Mac shows Kendra that life is for the living . . . and lips are made for kissing. But could she believe that he'd want her forever? Welcome back, Joyce!

Rounding the lineup in a big way is **T.S., I LOVE YOU,** LOVESWEPT #545, by Theresa Gladden. This emotionally vivid story captures that indefinable quality that makes a LOVESWEPT romance truly special. Heroine T. S. Winslow never forgot the boy who rescued her when she was a teenage runaway, the boy who was her first love.

Now, sixteen years later, circumstances have brought them together again, but old sorrows have made Logan Hunter vow never to give his heart. Theresa handles this tender story beautifully!

Look for four spectacular books on sale this month from FANFARE. First, **THE GOLDEN BARBARIAN,** by best-selling author Iris Johansen—here at last is the long-awaited historical prequel to the LOVESWEPT romances created by Iris about the dazzling world of Sedikhan. A sweeping novel set against the savage splendor of the desert, this is a stunningly sensual tale of passion and love between a princess and a sheik, two of the "founders" of Sedikhan. *Romantic Times* calls **THE GOLDEN BARBARIAN** ". . . an exciting tale . . . The sizzling tension . . . is the stuff which leaves an indelible mark on the heart." *Rendezvous* described it as ". . . a remarkable story you won't want to miss."

Critically acclaimed author Gloria Goldreich will touch your heart with **MOTHERS,** a powerful, moving portrait of two couples whose lives become intertwined through surrogate motherhood. What an eloquent and poignant tale about family, friendship, love, and the promise of new life.

LUCKY'S LADY, by ever-popular LOVESWEPT author Tami Hoag, is now available in paperback and is a must read! Those of you who fell in love with Remy Doucet in **RESTLESS HEART** will lose your heart once more to his brother, for bad-boy Cajun Lucky Doucet is one rough and rugged man of the bayou. And when he takes elegant Serena Sheridan through a Louisiana swamp to find her grandfather, they generate what *Romantic Times* has described as "enough steam heat to fog up any reader's glasses."

Finally, immensely talented Susan Bowden delivers a thrilling historical romance in **TOUCHED BY THORNS.** When a high-born beauty determined to reclaim her heritage strikes a marriage bargain with a daring Irish soldier, she never expects to succumb to his love, a love that would deny the English crown, and a deadly conspiracy.

And you can get these four terrific books only from FANFARE, where you'll find the best in women's fiction.

Also on sale this month in the Doubleday hardcover edition is **INTIMATE STRANGERS** by Alexandra Thorne. In this gripping contemporary novel, Jade Howard will slip into a flame-colored dress—and awake in another time, in another woman's life, in her home . . . and with her husband. Thoroughly absorbing, absolutely riveting!

Happy reading!

With warmest wishes,

Nita Taublib

Nita Taublib
Associate Publisher
FANFARE and LOVESWEPT

Don't miss these fabulous
Bantam Fanfare titles
on sale in MARCH.

THE GOLDEN BARBARIAN
by Iris Johansen

MOTHERS
by Gloria Goldreich

LUCKY'S LADY
by Tami Hoag

TOUCHED BY THORNS
by Susan Bowden

Ask for them by name.

On the following pages are excerpts from THE
GOLDEN BARBARIAN and LUCKY'S LADY
by Iris Johansen and Tami Hoag, two of your
favorite LOVESWEPT authors.

THE GOLDEN BARBARIAN
by Iris Johansen

Here is the timeless story of love and adventure set among hills of gold, warring tribes and fabled kingdoms—the story of a fearless princess and a barbarian sheikh . . .

Flaunting the oppressive destiny decreed for her by the kingdom of Tamrovia, Princess Theresa Christina Rubinoff struck a sensual bargain with a handsome barbarian chieftain. She vowed to play his seductive game, surrendering herself to his will, all the while determined to fight for her independence in a land that considered women only as playthings.

Mysterious as the desert night, rich as Midas, Galen Ben Raschid swept Tess away to his palace in exotic Sedikhan, offering her freedom in exchange for the marriage that would join their kingdoms. A man surrounded by enemies, he would make her a slave to his passion in order to bind her to his side, little knowing that when he took the captivating princess as his bride, he would lose his heart. . . .

In the following excerpt, Tess and the sheikh, now married, are returning to Sedikhan.

When Galen left the campfire and strolled around the pool toward the tent, it was nearly ten o'clock. Surprised, he stopped in front of Tess. "I thought you would have gone to sleep by now."

She scrambled to her feet. "I was tired, but not sleepy."

"Did Said furnish you with everything you needed?"

"Everything but sociable company." She added tartly, "Which you and Sacha certainly didn't deny yourself."

Galen held the tent flap back, and she preceded him inside. He took off his burnoose and tossed it on the cushions of a low divan. "I've been away for almost two weeks. Kalim had much to tell me."

"You didn't look as if you were conducting state business."

He turned to stare at her with raised brows. "That sounded suspiciously shrewish and wifely."

She flushed. "No such thing. I was curious . . . well, and

bored." She frowned. "I would have joined you, but the mere mention of doing such a thing sent Said into a tizzy."

"Quite rightly."

"Why? When members of the Tamrovian court travel, the women aren't stuck away in a hot, stuffy tent."

"You found the tent displeasing?"

"No." She looked around the tent. A thick, beautifully patterned carpet stretched over the ground, and everywhere her gaze wandered were colorful silk cushions, intricately worked brass lanterns, bejeweled silver candlesticks. "I've seen rooms at the palace that weren't as luxuriously furnished as this. "She went back to the primary subject. "But I don't like being imprisoned here."

"I'll consider ways to make it more palatable."

"But I don't want to stay here. Can't I join you in the evening around the campfire? If the court does not—"

"The men of your court haven't been without a woman for four weeks," he interrupted bluntly. "And your Tamrovian courtiers are tame as day-old pups compared to my tribesmen."

Her eyes widened. "They would insult me?"

"No. You belong to me. They would offer no insult. But they would look at you and grow hard and know pain."

Her skin burned. "Your words are crude."

"The fact is crude, and you must understand it. I will not make my men suffer needlessly."

"You would rather have me suffer." She scowled. "I would think you'd try to teach your men to control their responses. After all, I'm not that comely."

He smiled faintly. "I thought we'd settled the matter of your comeliness last night."

She had not thought her cheeks could get any hotter, but she found she was wrong. "Not everyone would find me to their taste. I think you must be a little peculiar."

He chuckled, and his face looked as boyish as it had when he'd laughed and joked with his men. "I assure you that my tastes are not at all unusual. You have a quality I've seen in few women."

She gazed at him warily. "What?"

"Life." His eyes held her own, and his expression suddenly sobered. "I've never met a woman so alive as you, *kilen.*"

Her stomach fluttered as she looked at him. She tore her gaze away from his face to stare down at the patterns in the carpet. "Your women are without spirit?"

"They have spirit," he said softly. "But they don't light up a tent by merely walking into it."

The flutter came again, and with it a strange breathlessness. "Pretty words. But what you're about to say is that I *must* stay in the tent."

"What I'm saying is that I prefer to save your light for myself."

Joy soared through her with bewildering intensity. She mustn't let him sway her feelings like this, she thought desperately. Sacha had said Galen gave whatever was demanded of him. Perhaps he thought this flattery was what she wanted of him. "As I said, pretty words." She changed the subject as she forced herself to lift her eyes to gaze directly at him. "You look different in your robe."

"More the barbarian?"

"I didn't say that," she said quickly.

"But you thought it." He smiled bitterly. "I've embraced many of your civilized Western ways, but I refuse to give up everything. The material of our robes is thin, comfortable, and the white reflects the sun." He strolled to the small trunk in the corner. "Which reminds me, you look most uncomfortably hot in your velvet riding habit. I think we must do something about it." He rummaged until he found another robe like the one he was wearing. "Here, put this on." He turned and tossed the garment to her. "You'll find it far more satisfactory."

"My habit is comfortable."

"And unattractive enough to satisfy me when you're out of the tent in the presence of my men." He met her gaze. "But not when we're alone. Put on the robe."

She was to dress herself to please him. She knew wives did such things, but the idea was somehow . . . intimate. The air between them changed, thickened. She was suddenly acutely conscious of the soft texture of the cotton robe in her hands, the sound of Said's flute weaving through the darkness, the intensity of Galen's expression as he gazed at her. She swallowed. "Very well." She began to undo the fastening at the throat of her brown habit.

He watched her for a minute before he turned and strode toward the entrance of the tent.

"You're leaving?" she asked, startled. "I thought—" She broke off, her tongue moistening her lower lip.

"You thought I would want to look at you again." He smiled. "I do. But it was easier last night at the inn, with all the trappings of civilization about me. Here, I'm freer and must take care." He lifted the flap of the tent, and the next moment she saw him standing outside, silhouetted by the moonlight against the vast dark sky.

He wasn't going to leave her. The rush of relief surging through her filled her with confusion and fear. Surely, the only reason she didn't want him to leave was because she had felt so alone in such a strange land, she assured herself. She couldn't really care if he went back to the tribesmen by the fire.

"*Dépêches-toi,*" he said softly, not looking at her.

Her hands flew, undoing the fastenings of the habit, and a few minutes after she was slipping naked into the softness of the robe.

It was far too large for her, the hem dragging the floor, the sleeves hanging ridiculously long. On her small frame the robe looked ludicrous and not at all seductive. She strode over to the trunk and rummaged until she found a black silk sash, wound the length three times around her waist, and tied it in a knot in front before before rolling up the sleeves to her elbows. The garment was so voluminous she should have felt uncomfortable, but the cotton was light as air compared to her habit. She ruffled her hair before stalking belligerently toward the opening of the tent. "I look foolish. You must promise not to laugh at me."

"Must I?" He continued to look at the campfire across the pond. "But laughter is so rare in this world."

"Well, I have no desire to provide you with more." She stopped beside him and scowled up at him. "I'm sure I don't look in the least what you intended. But it's your fault. I told you that I wasn't comely."

"So you did." His gaze shifted to her face and then down her draped body. His lips twitched. "You do look a trifle . . . overwhelmed." He sobered. "But you're wrong, it's exactly what I intended."

"Truly?" She frowned doubtfully. How could she be expected to gain understanding of the man when he changed from moment to moment? Last night he had wanted her without clothing, and now it appeared he desired her to be covered from chin to toes. She shrugged. "But you're right, this is much more comfortable than my habit."

"I'm glad you approve." His mouth turned up at the corners. "I should have hated to be proved wrong."

"You would never admit it. Men never do. My father—"

He frowned. "I find I'm weary of being compared to your father."

She could certainly understand his distaste. "I'm sorry," she said earnestly. I know few men, so perhaps I'm being unfair. I can see how you would object to being tossed in the same stable as my father, for he's not at all pleasant."

He started to smile, and then his lips thinned. "No, not at all pleasant." He reached out and touched her hair with a gentle hand. "But you don't have to worry about him any longer, *kilen*."

"I don't worry about him." She shrugged. "It would be a waste of time to worry about things I can't change. It's much more sensible to accept the bad and enjoy the good in life."

"Much more sensible." His fingers moved from her hair to brush the shadows beneath her eyes. "I drove us at a cruel pace from Dinar. Was the day hard for you?"

Her flesh seemed to tingle beneath his touch, filling her with the same excitement and panic she had known the night before. She had to force herself not to step away from him. "No, I would not admit to being so puny. I did not sleep well last night." She had not meant to blurt that out, she thought vexedly. "I mean—"

"I know what you mean. I did not sleep well either." Galen turned her around and shoved her gently toward the tent. "Which is why I pushed the pace today. I wanted to be weary enough to sleep tonight. Good night, *kilen*."

"Aren't you coming?"

"Presently. Go to bed."

She wanted to argue, but there was something about the tension of the back he turned toward her that gave her pause. Still, for some reason she hesitated, reluctant to leave him. "What time do we leave tomorrow?"

"At dawn."

"And how long will it take to get to Zalandan?"

"Another five days."

"Will we—"

"Go to bed, Tess!"

The suppressed violence in his voice made her jump and start hurriedly toward the entrance of the tent. "Oh, very well." She entered the tent and then slowed her pace to a deliberate stroll as she moved toward the curtained sleeping area. After all, there was nothing to run away from when Galen was not even in pursuit.

She drew back the thin curtain and the next moment sank onto the cushions heaped on the low, wide divan. There was much to say for barbarism, she thought as she burrowed into the silken pillows. This divan was much more comfortable than the bed at the inn. . . .

Tess's curly hair was garnet-dark flame against the beige satin of the pillow under her head. His robe had worked open revealing her delicate shoulder, the skin of which was soft as velvet and even more luminescent than the satin of the pillow below it.

As Galen watched, she stirred, half turned, and a beautifully formed limb emerged from the cotton folds of the robe. Not a voluptuous thigh but a strong, well-muscled one.

Exquisite. He felt a painful thickening in his groin as he stood looking at her. He had deliberately provided her with the oversized garment to avoid seeing her naked as he had last night, but somehow this half nudity was even more arousing.

It was because he was back in Sedikhan, he told himself. It couldn't be this half-woman, half-child who was causing his physical turmoil. He always felt a seething unrest and wildness when he was on home ground. The memories of his past debaucheries were to vivid to be ignored when he was back in the desert. But the wildness had never been this strong, the urge to take a woman so violent. . . .

But he could control it. He had to control it.

Why? She was only a woman, like any other.

No, not like any other. She had a man's sense of honor. She had made a bargain and would keep it. He could have her simply by reaching out a hand. He could put his palm on those soft, springy curls surrounding her womanhood and stroke her as he did Selik. He could pluck at that delicious secret nub until she screamed for satisfaction. He could pull her to her knees and make—

Make. The word cooled his fever for her. Only a true barbarian used force on women.

He stripped quickly, blew out the candle in the copper lantern hanging on the tent pole, and settled down on the cushions beside Tess, careful not to touch her. The heaviness in his loins turned painful. He lay with his back to her, his heart pounding against his rib cage.

He could control it. He was no savage to take—

He felt the cushions shift. The scent of lavender and woman drifted over him, and he tried to breathe shallowly to mitigate its effect.

Then he felt her fingers in his hair.

Every muscle in his body went rigid. "Tess?"

She murmured something drowsily, only half-awake, her fingers caressing his nape.

"What"—a shudder racked through him as her fingertips brushed his shoulders—"are you doing?"

She pulled the ribbon from his queue and tossed it aside. "Wife's duty . . ."

She moved away again, and the rhythm of her breathing told him she was sound asleep once more.

Wife's duty? Galen would have laughed if he hadn't been in the grip of hot frustration. He would like to show her a wife's "duty." He would like to move between her thighs and plunge deep. He would like to take her for a ride in the desert *coït de cheval*, cradling her buttocks in his palms, making her feel every inch of him. He would like to— He forced himself to abandon such thoughts and to unclench his fists.

He had put his wild days behind him. He could no longer take with reckless abandon. He must think, consider, wait.

Dear God in heaven, he was hurting.

LUCKY'S LADY
by Tami Hoag

As wild and mysterious as the Louisiana swamp he called home, Lucky Doucet was an infuriatingly attractive Cajun no woman could handle. He believed there was no room in his solitary life for the likes of elegant Serena Sheridan, but he couldn't deny her desperate need to find her missing grandfather. He would help her but nothing more—yet once he felt the lure of the flaxen-haired beauty, an adventurer like Lucky couldn't resist playing with fire for long.

Serena felt unnerved, aroused, and excited by the ruggedly sexy renegade whose gaze burned her with its heat, but did she dare tangle with a rebel whose intensity was overwhelming, who claimed his heart was a no-man's land?

In the following excerpt, Lucky is taking Serena to his house in the swamp . . . to spend the night.

"Me, I'd say there's a lotta things here you don' understand, sugar," Lucky drawled.

Not the least of which was *him*, Serena thought, plucking at the edge of the mosquito netting. The man was a jumble of contradictions. Mean to her one minute and throwing mosquito netting over her the next; telling her in one breath he didn't involve himself in other people's affairs, then giving his commentary on the situation. She wouldn't have credited him with an abundance of compassion, but he was rescuing her from having to spend the night outside, and, barring nefarious reasons, compassion was the only motive she could see.

She wondered what kind of place he was taking her to. She didn't hold out much hope for luxurious accommodations. Her idea of a poacher's lair was just a notch above a cave with animal hides scattered over the floor. She pictured a tar-paper shack and a mud yard littered with dead electricity generators and discarded butane tanks. There would probably be a tumbledown shed full of poaching paraphernalia, racks of stolen pelts and buckets of rancid muskrat remains. She couldn't imagine Lucky hanging curtains. He struck her as the sort of man who would pin up centerfolds from raunchy magazines on the walls and call it art.

They rounded a bend in the bayou, and a small, neat house came into view. It was set on a tiny hillock in an alcove that had been cleared of trees. Its weathered-cypress siding shimmered pale silver in the fading light. It was a house in the old Louisiana country style, an Acadian house built on masonry piers to keep it above the damp ground. Steps led onto a deep gallery that was punctuated by shuttered windows and a screen door. An exterior staircase led up from the gallery to the overhanging attic that formed the ceiling of the gallery—a classic characteristic of Cajun architecture. Slim wooden columns supporting the overhang gave the little house a gracious air.

Serena was delightfully surprised to see something so neat and civilized in the middle of such a wilderness, but nothing could have surprised her more than to hear Lucky tell her it was his.

He scowled at the look of utter shock she directed up at him through the mosquito netting. "What'sa matter, *chère?* You were expecting some old white-trash shack with a yard full of pigs and chickens rootin' through the garbage?"

"Stop putting words in my mouth," she grumbled, unwilling to admit her unflattering thoughts, no matter how obvious they might have been.

A corner of Lucky's mouth curled upward, and his heavy-lidded eyes focused on her lips with the intensity of lasers. "Is there something else you want me to put there?"

Serena's heart thudded traitorously at the involuntary images that flitted through her mind. It was all she could do to keep her gaze from straying to the part of his anatomy that was at her eye level.

"You've really cornered the market on arrogance, haven't you?" she said, as disgusted with herself as she was with him.

"Me?" he said innocently, tapping a fist to his chest. "*Non.* I just know what a woman really wants, that's all."

"I'm sure you don't have the vaguest idea what a woman really wants," Serena said as she untangled herself from the *baire* and tossed it aside. She offered Lucky her hand as if she were a queen, and allowed him to hand her up onto the dock, giving him a smug smile as her feet settled on the solid wood. "But if you want to go practice your theory on yourself, don't let me stop you."

Lucky watched her walk away, perversely amused by her sass. She was limping slightly, but that didn't detract from the alluring sway of the backside that filled her snug white pants to heart-shaped perfection. Desire coiled like a spring in his gut. He might not have known what Miss Sheridan really wanted, but he damn well knew what his body wanted.

It was going to be a long couple of days.

He pulled the pirogue up out of the water and left it with its cargo of suitcases and crawfish to join Serena on the gallery. He didn't like having her there. This place revealed things about him. Having her there allowed her to get too close when his defenses were demanding to keep her an emotional mile away. He might have wanted her physically, but that was as far as it went. He had learned the hard way not to let anyone inside the walls he had painstakingly built around himself. He would have been safer if she could have gone on believing he lived like an animal in some ancient rusted-out house trailer.

"It's very nice," she said politely as he trudged up the steps onto the gallery.

"It's just a house," he growled, jerking the screen door open. "Go in and sit down. I'm gonna take the sliver out of that foot of yours before gangrene sets in."

Serena bared her teeth at him a parody of a smile. "Such a gracious host," she said, sauntering in ahead of him.

The interior of the house was as much of a surprise to her as the exterior had been. It consisted of two large rooms, both visible from the entrance—a kitchen and dining area, and a bedroom and living area. The place was immaculate. There was no pile of old hunting boots, no stacks of old porno magazines, no mountains of laundry, no litter of food-encrusted pots and pans. From what Serena could see on her initial reconnaissance, there wasn't as much as a dust bunny on the floor.

Lucky struck a match and lit a pair of kerosene lamps on the dining table, flooding the room with buttery-soft light, then left the room without a word. Serena pulled out a chair and sat down, still marveling. His decorating style was austere, as spare and plain as an Amish home, a style that made the house itself seem like a work of art. The walls had a wainscoting of varnished cypress paneling beneath soft white plaster. The furnishings appeared to be meticulously restored antiques—a wide-plank cypress dining table, a large French armoire that stood against the wall, oak and hickory chairs with rawhide seats. In the kitchen area mysterious bunches of plants had been hung by their stems from a wide beam to dry. Ropes of garlic and peppers adorned the window above the sink in lieu of a curtain.

Lucky appeared to approve of refrigeration and running water, but not electric lights. Another contradiction. It made Serena vaguely uncomfortable to think there was so much more to him than she had been prepared to believe. It would have been easy to dislike a man who lived in a hovel and poached for a living. This house and its contents put him in a whole other light—one he didn't particularly like to have her see him in, if the look on his face was any indication.

He emerged with first aid supplies cradled in one brawny arm from what she assumed was a bathroom. These he set on the table, then he pulled up a chair facing hers and jerked her foot up onto his lap, nearly pulling her off her seat. He tossed her shoe aside and gave her bare foot a ferocious look, lifting it to eye level and turning it to capture the best light. Serena clutched the arm of her chair with one hand and the edge of the table with the other, straining against tipping over backward. She winced as Lucky prodded at the sliver.

"Stubborn as that grandpapa of yours, walkin' around half the day with this in your foot," he grumbled, playing the tweezers. "*Espèsces de tête dure.*"

"What does that mean? Ouch!"

"You're a hardheaded thing."

"Ouch" She tried to jerk her foot back.

"Be still!"

"You sadist!"

"Quit squirming!"

"Ou-ou-ouch!"

"Got it."

She felt an instant of blessed relief as soon as the splinter was out of her foot, but it was short-lived. Serena hissed through her teeth at the first sting of the alcohol, blinking furiously at the tears that automatically rose in her eyes.

"Your bedside manner leaves a lot to be desired," she said harshly.

Lucky raised his eyes and stared at her over her toes. The corners of his mouth turned up. "Yeah, but my manner *in* bed won't leave anything to be desired. I can promise you that, *chère.*"

Serena met his hypnotic gaze, her heart beating a wild pulse in her throat as his long fingers gently traced the bones of her foot and ankle. All thoughts of pain vanished from her head. Desire coursed through her veins in a sudden hot stream that both excited and frightened her. She didn't react this way to men. She certainly shouldn't have been reacting his way to *this* man. What had become of her common sense? What had become of her control?

With an effort she found her voice, but it was soft and smoky and she barely recognized it when she spoke. "That's no promise, that's a threat."

Lucky eased her foot down and rose slowly. His fingers curled around the arms of Serena's chair and he tilted it back on its hind legs, his eyes never leaving hers as he leaned down close.

"Is it?" he said in a silken whisper, his mouth inches from hers. "Are you afraid of me, *chère*?"

"No," she said, the tremor in her voice making a mockery of her answer. She stared at him, eyes wide, her breath escaping in a thin stream from between her parted lips. The molten heat in his gaze stirred an answering warmth inside her and she found herself suddenly staring at his mouth, that incredibly sensuous, beautifully carved mouth.

"You're not afraid of me?" he said, arching a brow, the words barely audible. He leaned closer still. "Then mebbe this is what you're afraid of."

He closed the distance between them, touching his lips to hers.

The heat was instantaneous. It burst around them and inside them, as bright and hot as the flare of the lamps on the table beside them. Serena sucked in a little gasp, drawing Lucky closer. He settled his mouth against hers, telling himself he wanted just a taste of her, nothing more, but fire swept through him, his blood scalding his veins. One taste. Just one taste . . . would never be enough.

Her mouth was like silk soaked in wine—soft, sweet, intoxicating. His tongue slipped between her parted lips to better savor the experience. He stroked and explored and Serena responded in kind, reacting on instinct. Her tongue slid sinuously against Lucky's. His plunged deeper into her mouth. The flames leapt higher.

A moan drifted up from Serena's throat, and her arms slid up around Lucky's neck. She could feel herself growing dizzy, as if her body were floating up out of the chair. Dimly she realized Lucky was rising and pulling her up with him. His arms banded around her like steel, lifting her, pulling her close. His big hands slid down to the small of her back and pressed her into him.

He was fully aroused. His erection pressed into her belly, as hard as granite, as tempting as sin. She arched against it wantonly, reacting without thought. A growl rumbled deep in his chest, and he rolled his hips against her as he changed the angle of the kiss and plunged his tongue into her mouth again and again.

He stroked a hand down over the full swell of one hip. Cupping her buttock, he lifted her to bring her feminine mound up against his hardness. She made a small, frightened sound in her throat and need surged through him like a flood. He wanted her. God, he wanted her! He wanted to take her right here, right now, on the table, on the floor. It was madness.

Madness.

Sweet heaven, what was he doing? he wondered, finally hearing the alarm bells clanging in his head. What was she doing to him? He set her away from him with a violence that made her stumble back against the chair she'd been sitting in. She stared at him, her eyes wide and dark with a seductive mix of passion and fear. Her hair tumbled around her shoulders in golden disarray. Her mouth, swollen and red from the force of his kiss, trembled. She stared at him as if he were something wild and terrifying.

Wild was exactly what he was feeling—out of control, beyond the reach of reason. His chest was heaving like a bellows as he tried to draw in enough oxygen to think straight. He speared his hands into his hair and hung his head, closing his eyes. Control. He needed control.

Control. She'd lost control—of the situation, of herself. Serena swallowed hard and pressed a hand to her bruised lips. How could this have happened? She didn't even *like* the man. But the instant his mouth had touched hers she had experienced an explosion of desire that had melted everything else. She hadn't thought of anything but his mouth on hers, the taste of him, the strength of his arms, the feel of his body. Shivers rocked through her now like the aftershocks of an earthquake. Heaven help her, she didn't know herself anymore. What had become of her calm self-discipline, her training, her ability to distance herself from a situation and examine it analytically?

You wanted him, Serena. How's that for analysis?

She shook her head a little in stunned disbelief. "I think I would have been safer with the coon hounds," she mumbled.

Something flashed in Lucky's eyes. His expression went cold. "*Non.* You're safe in this house, lady. I'm out of here."

He turned and stormed into the next room. There was a banging of doors that made Serena wince. When he reappeared he was wearing a black T-shirt that hugged his chest like a coat of paint. He shrugged on a shoulder holster. The pistol it cradled oked big enough to bring down an elephant. Serena felt her eyes iden and her jaw drop.

"It's not hunting season." She didn't realize she had spoken loud, but Lucky turned and gave her a long, very disturbing look, is panther's eyes glowing beneath his heavy dark brows.

"It is for what I'm after," he said in a silky voice.

He pulled the gun and checked the load. The clip slid back into ace with a smooth, sinister hiss and click. Then he was gone. le slipped out the door like a shadow, without a sound.

Serena felt the hair rise up on the back of her neck. For a long oment she stood there, frozen with fear in the heat of the night. /ith an effort she finally forced her feet to move and went to the creen door to look out.

The night was as black as fresh tar with only a sliver of moon iining down on the bayou. The water gleamed like a sheet of ass. She thought she caught a glimpse of Lucky poling his rogue out toward a stand of cypress, but in a blink he was gone, anished, as if he were a creature from the darkest side of the ight, able to appear and disappear at will.

"Heaven help me," she whispered, brushing her fingertips cross her bottom lip. "What have I gotten myself into now?"

MOTHERS
by Gloria Goldreich

MOTHERS is the story of two couples who have happy marriages in common—but very little else. Nina and David Roth live an affluent suburban life. Stacey and Hall Cosgrove, who have been married since high school, face a future of scraping to get by. There's another difference: the Cosgroves have three children; the Roths cannot conceive. One obstetrician knows of the Roth's desperate wish for a child, just as he knows how easily Stacey Cosgrove is able to conceive—and how much her family needs money. A financial agreement is made for Stacey to carry David's child. However, what starts out as a business arrangement cannot remain simple when human lives are involved. A rare bond of shared motherhood forms between the two women, but as the birth nears, an event occurs that breaks all their careful preparations apart. . . .

TOUCHED BY THORNS
by Susan Bowden

For seventeen idyllic years, lovely, strong-willed Katherine Radcliffe, heroine of TOUCHED BY THORNS, had led a charmed existence on her family's estate in Yorkshire. Suddenly, in one night of shattering tragedy, her beloved Radcliffe Manor is lost to her. Betrayed, then imprisoned, she is rescued by the handsome, mysterious Captain Brendan Fitzgerald, a distant cousin and now rightful heir to Radcliffe Manor. Mesmerized by Katherine's uncommon beauty and fiery disposition, he falls deeply in love and strikes a marriage "bargain" to which she, determined to regain Radcliffe at any cost, reluctantly agrees. Slowly, almost against her will, she finds herself succumbing to Brendan's tenderness and the fierce passions she senses lie just beneath the surface of his gallant demeanor.

FANFARE

On Sale in APRIL

THE FIREBIRDS

☐ 29613-2 $4.99/5.99 in Canada
by Beverly Byrne

author of THE MORGAN WOMEN

The third and final book in Beverly Byrne's remarkable trilogy of passion and revenge. The fortunes of the House of Mendoza are stunningly resolved in this contemporary romance.

FORTUNE'S CHILD

☐ 29424-5 $5.50/6.50 in Canada
by Pamela Simpson

Twenty years ago, Christina Fortune disappeared. Now she's come home to claim what's rightfully hers. But is she an heiress . . . or an imposter?

SEASON OF SHADOWS

☐ 29589-6 $5.99/6.99 in Canada
by Mary Mackey

Lucy and Cassandra were polar opposites, but from the first day they met they became the best of friends. Roommates during the turbulent sixties, they stood beside each other through fiery love affairs and heartbreaking loneliness.